A CERTAIN SMILE

ABOUT THE AUTHOR

FRANÇOISE Sagan (Françoise Quoirez, 1935–2004) was a French novelist, playwright, and screenwriter, best known for her novel *Bonjour Tristesse*, published in 1954 when she was eighteen, and later made into a film directed by Otto Preminger in 1958. Sagan attended the Sorbonne in Paris, but did not graduate. She became popular among disillusioned youths of the time, who identified with the young, bored, lonely characters in her novels. Sagan's other novels, many of which were translated into English, include *Those Without Shadows*, *La Chamade*, *The Wonderful Clouds*, and *Aimez-vous Brahms?* Several of her novels were later adapted for film, and her own life has been made the subject of Diane Kurys's film *Sagan*.

FRANÇOISE SAGAN

A Certain Smile

A NOVEL

Translated from the French by Anne Green

With a New Foreword by
Diane Johnson

THE UNIVERSITY OF CHICAGO PRESS

The University of Chicago Press, Chicago, 60637
Translation by Anne Green copyright, ©,
    1956, by E. P. Dutton & Co., Inc.
All rights reserved.
University of Chicago Press edition 2011
Printed in the United States of America
Originally published in French by Éditions Julliard, Paris, in 1956.

20 19 18 17 16 15 14 13 12 11   1 2 3 4 5

ISBN-13: 978-0-226-73347-0 (paper)
ISBN-10: 0-226-73347-5 (paper)

Library of Congress Cataloging-in-Publication Data:

Sagan, Françoise, 1935–2004.
    [Certain sourire. English]
    A certain smile : a novel / Françoise Sagan ; translated from the
French by Anne Green ; with a new foreword by Diane Johnson.
        p. cm.
    ISBN-13: 978-0-226-73347-0 (pbk. : alk. paper)
    ISBN-10: 0-226-73347-5 (pbk. : alk. paper)
    1. Title.
    PQ2633.U74C413 2011
    843'.914—dc22
                    2011010517

♾ This paper meets the requirements of ANSI / NISO
z39.48-1992 (Permanence of Paper).

To Florence Malraux

Love is what happens between two lovers.

ROGER VAILLAND

FOREWORD

By Diane Johnson

WHEN the eighteen-year-old Françoise Sagan published her best-known novel, *Bonjour Tristesse*, in 1954, it became a phenomenon, hugely successful both in France and in America, as much for the youth of the author as for its undoubted charm. Critics and readers alike admired its artistry, concision, lapidary language, and fashionable cynicism. It was doubted, however, that the gifted young author could repeat her precocious feat.

She proceeded to do exactly that with *A Certain Smile*, published in 1956, which she is said to have written in two months. Many found it to be the superior book and preferred it to *Bonjour Tristesse*, finding it less melodramatic, newly compassionate, equally wise, and more realistic, while it exhibited, of course, the same fashionable ennui that readers of the earlier book had found so luridly fascinating. Cecile, the heroine of *Bonjour Tristesse*, whose antics interfere with and blight her playboy father's love affairs, imagines herself to be blasé and adult. She remains unaware of her own oedipal problems and fails to reach the self-understanding that would provide a more satisfactory denouement.

But Dominique, the narrator of *A Certain Smile*, another gamine of eighteen or nineteen, does come to certain, more mature conclusions after her unhappy affair with her boy-friend's uncle Luc. Attracting a desirable older man prompts her to observe that her idea of herself, "which had always reflected such a very poor image of me, might be a little too severe and pessimistic, after all" (52–54). Has the tender question of what would now be called self-esteem ever been better described, the true origins of her love for Luc more delicately suggested? The ending is both more satisfying and psychologically more convincing, while the writing is if anything more assured.

Both novels, like the novels Sagan would go on to write (*Aimez-vous Brahms?*, *La Chamade*—twenty in all), are distinguished by their brilliant descriptions and incisive power of putting the most complicated psychological states into nutshell phrases. And she had the rare ability to summarize and understand an experience, it seemed, while she was going through it—like Dominique, her protagonist, but unlike most writers, who can only look back and report on their own experiences after a decade or more. Reviewers at the time it was first published even used the term *monstre*, monster, to describe her odd detachment.

Her narrators, like, perhaps, Sagan herself, are never free of the sense that they are watching themselves from some remove high above. Dominique loves her boyfriend Bernard, but, as she says, "I was fated, because of something within me, to follow a young man's closely shaven neck, to let myself be marched off, unresisting, with a host of little thoughts of my own, as cold and slippery as fish" (11).

In first-person stories more than in those written in the more usual third-person voice, we feel the presence of the writer herself behind the "I" of the narrator. And while a writer can create a narrator more stupid or bewildered than herself, she obviously can't make her more clever or more brilliant, so that those unsurpassable qualities in a character tend to stick to the author too; thus Dominique merges into our sense of Sagan, both persons of unusual penetration, and the Dominique that Sagan creates seems more a clever and observant avatar than an independent character like, say, Scrooge or Jean Valjean. Which of them, Sagan or Dominique, wonders, "What can any human being think about on an empty beach, facing an empty sea, beside someone who is sleeping?" (84); or says, "Happiness has no history" (82)? Both, of course, have these writerly thoughts.

Sagan abetted the autobiographical impression given by her works with her personal behavior off the page, that of a troubled celebrity with all the trappings—lovers (both male and female), honors, gambling debts, car wrecks, tax problems, and drugs. She died at the age of sixty-nine in 2004, so much a creature of her period that one wonders what kind of turn her works would have had to take if they were written today. Readers of novels from the 1950s—or from any earlier period, such as the Victorian—must make certain allowances for period details. Barely on the cusp of sexual freedom then, heroines were not free of fears of pregnancy, as when Dominique has a moment of nausea and tells herself, "That's it! The nightmare which I knew all too well for having been through it, mistakenly, many times before had come back to haunt me" (58).

Pregnancy was a frequent recourse of fifties fiction. Now in the days of modern contraception and altered mores, Sagan's book would be quite different—Dominique and Luc would be in bed at the first possible moment, and the long, agonizing frissons of anticipation the French novel has so long depended on, and the subtle courtship or the drawn-out process of rupture, as in *Adolphe*, or Colette's novels, or even *La Princesse de Clèves*, are lost to modern novelists. To say nothing of the smoking, detailed on every page, which is likely to complicate the response of the modern reader with unwanted associations of smelly ashtrays and lung cancer.

Besides the details of love, boredom was the watchword of the existentialist period. Reading now of their boredom, one wonders what they really meant by their excessive world-weariness? When Luc says, "We'd be very happy, very tender; I'd introduce you to the sea, to money and the freedom it brings. We'd be much less bored. There you have it" (53), or when he says that though he has a lot of work to do, "it didn't interest him particularly," and she has the "necessity of delving deeper into subjects which had bored me the year before" (88), are they adopting the same discouragement, the same weariness, that they might have been reading about in Sartre's *La Nausée*, a kind of fashionable alienation typical of the time, an attitude intellectuals were expected to strike? The question of whether all this boredom is rhetorical or reflects the way they really felt must remain mysterious to the reader of a half century later, but because it seems to be authentic—to borrow another byword of the period—its poignancy is as fresh for us as it was then, and its tragic effects on the lives of people and characters then lend a dimension our more satiric age seems to lack.

A CERTAIN SMILE

Chapter 1

W E had spent the afternoon
in a café on the Rue Saint-Jacques, a spring afternoon
just like any other. I felt bored, after a fashion; I
wandered from the juke box to the window, while
Bertrand talked about the course given by Spire. At a
certain point I leaned against the machine and watched
the record rise slowly, then slant down to meet the
needle, almost tenderly, like a cheek. For some reason
a terrific feeling of happiness swept over me; I had an
overwhelming intuition that some day I was going to
die, that my hand would be gone from this chromium
edge and the sun from my sight.

I turned toward Bertrand. He was looking at me and
got up when he saw me smile. He wouldn't let me be
happy without him. My only moments of happiness
were to be those which we lived most closely together.
I was already vaguely aware of this, but now I couldn't
stand it any longer and turned away. The piano
sketched the theme of *Lone and Sweet*; a clarinet took
it up and I knew every note.

I had met Bertrand the year before, while we were
both taking examinations. We lived through an anxious

week, side by side, before I went off to spend the summer with my parents. The last evening he kissed me. Then he wrote me letters. At first rather casually. Then his tone changed. I had an intermittently feverish reaction to these successive stages, so that when he wrote: "I think this is a ridiculous statement, but I believe I love you," I was able to reply truthfully, in the same tone: "This is a ridiculous statement, but I love you, too." This answer came to me naturally, or rather, as an echo.

My parents' place on the Yonne River offered little to do. I used to go down to the river bank, look for a while at the formations of swaying yellow algae on the surface and then skip worn, flat stones, which moved as swiftly as swallows, across the water. All summer I repeated "Bertrand" over and over, projecting the name both within myself and into the future. It was like me to set the key of a relationship by means of letters.

Now Bertrand was standing behind me. He handed me my glass and when I turned around I found myself close to him. He was always a little annoyed by the fact that I took no part in the discussions. I liked to read, but literary talk bored me. That was something he couldn't get used to.

"You always play the same record," he said. "Don't get me wrong; I like it."

He said the last sentence in a noncommittal voice, and I remembered that we had heard the record for the first time together. I was always coming up against such little sentimental outbursts, references to events in our liaison of which I had no recollection. "He's nothing to me," I thought suddenly. "He bores me stiff. I feel so completely indifferent. I'm nothing myself, either, nothing, absolutely nothing." Once more the same absurd, rapturous emotion caught at my throat.

"I've got to go see my uncle, the one that spends so much time abroad," said Bertrand. "Do you want to come along?"

He went out first, and I followed. I didn't know his uncle, the traveler, and had no particular desire to meet him. But I was fated, because of something within me, to follow a young man's closely shaven neck, to let myself be marched off, unresisting, with a host of little thoughts of my own, as cold and slippery as fish, and yet with a certain tender sensation. As we walked down the boulevard together our feet were in as perfect step as our bodies at night. He held my hand, and we were as slim and attractive as a couple in a magazine illustration.

All along the boulevard and on the platform of the bus that took us to his uncle, the globe-trotter, I liked Bertrand very well. When the jolts threw me against him, he laughed and put a protective arm around me. I leaned against his coat, just at the curve of his shoulder, this masculine shoulder where my head fitted so well. I breathed in the smell of him, which was so very familiar and yet never failed to stir my feelings. Bertrand was my first lover, and it was on his body that I had discovered the odor of mine. It's always through someone else's body that, first warily and then with a rush of gratitude, you discover your own, its length, its smell. . . .

Bertrand was talking about his uncle, the traveler, for whom he seemed to have no great liking. He told me about his uncle's trips, which he considered more or less of a sham. Bertrand spent his time uncovering other people's pretenses; he was so analytical that he went about half fearful that, without his realizing it, his own life, too, was an empty cover-up. This struck me as very funny, and my amusement rubbed him the wrong way.

Bertrand's uncle was waiting for him at a table outside a café. As soon as I saw him I said to Bertrand that he didn't look so bad, after all. By this time he was getting up to greet us.

"Luc," said Bertrand, "I've brought a friend, Dominique. . . . Dominique, this is my Uncle Luc, the great traveler."

I was agreeably surprised and said to myself: "Quite presentable, this uncle." He had gray eyes and a tired, somewhat sad expression. In his way, he was actually good-looking.

"What about your last trip?" asked Bertrand. "How did it go?"

"Very badly. I had to wind up an estate in Boston. Dusty little lawyers in every corner. Altogether very tiresome. And what about you?"

"In two months we'll be having our exams," replied Bertrand.

He lingered over the "our." That was the conjugal side of the Sorbonne. Exams were like so many babies.

The uncle turned toward me: "Do you have exams, too?"

"Yes," I said vaguely. (My activities, no matter how unimportant, always made me feel slightly ashamed.)

"I'm out of cigarettes," said Bertrand.

He got up, and I looked after him as he went out. Every now and then I realized that this combination of muscles, reflexes and brown skin belonged to me, and it always seemed a most amazing piece of luck.

"And what do you do with yourself, aside from having examinations?" the uncle asked me.

"Nothing," I replied, "or at least, nothing much."

I raised my hand to show discouragement. He seized it in mid-air, and I looked at him, disconcerted. In the space of a split second I thought to myself: "I like him. He's a bit old, and I like him." He laid my hand on the table and said with a smile: "Your fingers are full of ink, and that's a very good sign. You'll pass your exams and turn into a brilliant lawyer, although you don't seem very talkative."

We both laughed. I wanted him to be my friend.

But Bertrand was back, and Luc was talking to him. I didn't listen. Luc had a slow voice and large hands. I thought to myself: "He's just the kind that seduces little girls like me." I was already on my guard, but not sufficiently to avoid feeling a little stab of vexation when he asked us to come to lunch—with him and his wife—two days later.

Chapter 2

I SPENT two rather boring days before lunching at Luc's house. After all, what did I have to do? To work over an examination that wouldn't lead me anywhere in particular, to loaf about in the sun and to let Bertrand make love to me, without my giving him anything very deep in return. I was really fond of him, just the same. Trust, esteem and tenderness were not to be despised, and I thought very little about passion. This absence of genuine feeling seemed to me the most normal way to live. Living, after all, meant contriving to be as contented as humanly possible, and that was not easy.

I lived in a kind of boardinghouse for women students. The landlady was broad-minded and I could quite safely come home at one or two in the morning. My room was large, low-ceilinged and completely bare, since my early schemes for decoration had petered out long ago. All I asked of my surroundings was that they should not disturb me. The whole house had a provincial flavor which was very much to my liking. My window looked out on a courtyard enclosed by a low wall. Above this there squatted the much maligned, fragmentary Paris sky, which opened up here and there, over a balcony or street, in a most moving fashion.

I got up in the morning, went to classes, and met Bertrand for lunch. Then there were the Sorbonne library, movies, work, friends and outdoor cafés. In the evening we danced, or else we went to Bertrand's room, where we stretched out on the bed, made love and then talked for hours in the dark. I was happy enough, but inside me, like a warm, living animal, there was a feeling of boredom, loneliness and occasionally of exhilaration. I thought there must be something wrong with my liver.

That Friday, before going to Luc's house for lunch, I paid a half-hour visit to Catherine. Catherine was lively, domineering and always in love. I had not chosen her friendship; it had been imposed upon me. She considered me frail and defenseless, and this attitude I could and did enjoy. Sometimes I thought she was quite marvelous. My indifference became poetical in her eyes, just as it had been in Bertrand's, before he was seized with a sudden and compelling desire to possess me.

That day Catherine was in love with a cousin, and told me all about it. I told her that I was lunching with some of Bertrand's family, and at that very moment I realized that Luc had somewhat slipped out of my mind. Too bad. Why didn't I have some interminable and ingenuous love story to match with hers? But my silence did not surprise her. We were already frozen into our allotted roles: she talking, while I listened; she giving advice, while I closed my ears.

This visit depressed me. I went to Luc's without much enthusiasm, in fact with a certain amount of terror. I should have to talk, make myself agreeable, build up a picture of myself in their eyes. I should have liked to lunch alone, twiddling a mustard pot between my fingers, and to be vague, but completely. . . .

When I reached Luc's house, Bertrand was already there. He introduced me to his uncle's wife. There was a wonderful bloom on her face, something kind and at the same time beautiful. She was tall, blond and a trifle heavy; beautiful, yes, but not aggressively so. I thought to myself that she was the kind of woman many men would like to have for keeps, a woman that would make them happy, a gentle woman. Was I gentle? That was a question for Bertrand to answer. Of course, I held his hand, I never raised my voice, I stroked his hair. But then I hated to raise my voice and my hands liked his hair, which was warm and thick, like that of an animal.

Françoise was friendly to me from the start. She showed me over the luxurious apartment, gave me a drink and settled me in an armchair, all with wonderful courtesy and ease. The embarrassment I felt over my somewhat worn, out-of-shape sweater and skirt faded away. We waited for Luc, who was working. I realized that I should show some interest in Luc's profession, although such things meant nothing to me. I always wanted to ask people: "Are you in love? What are you reading?" But I never bothered about their profession, important as it might be to them.

"You look worried," said Françoise, smiling. "Will you have a little more whisky?"

"With pleasure."

"Dominique has a reputation for hard drinking," said Bertrand. "Do you know why?"

He jumped up and came over to me, with an important air.

"Her upper lip is a bit short; when she closes her eyes and drinks, it gives her an intense expression, which has no connection with the Scotch whatsoever."

As he spoke he took my upper lip between his thumb and forefinger and showed me off to Françoise as if I were a puppy. I began to laugh and he let me go. Just then Luc came into the room. When I saw him I thought once more, but this time with a stab of pain, that he was very handsome. It really hurt me, like everything, that he was not mine for the taking. There weren't so many things I wanted to take, but now I thought all at once that I should like to catch his face in my hands and squeeze it violently between my fingers, to press his full, rather wide lips to mine. Luc was not really handsome, as I was often to be told later on. But something about his features made this face, which I had seen only twice, a thousand times less foreign to me and a thousand times more desirable than Bertrand's, which I actually liked so very well.

Luc came in, greeted us and sat down. He could

remain astonishingly still. There was something tense and controlled in his deliberate gestures and relaxed body which I found infinitely disquieting. He looked tenderly at Françoise and I looked at him. I have forgotten what we said, but I know that Bertrand and Françoise were keeping up the conversation. Actually, it somewhat disgusts me to call up these preliminaries. At that moment, with a little caution and a little distance between us, I could have escaped him. On the other hand, I am anxious to get to the time when he first made me happy. The thought of describing those first moments, of momentarily shattering the flatness of mere words, fills me with bitter and impatient joy.

So we had lunch with Luc and Françoise. Afterward, in the street, I adapted my step to Luc's, which was rapid, and forgot Bertrand's. Luc took my elbow every time we crossed a street, and I remember how I found this embarrassing. I didn't know what to do with my forearm, or with the hand that hung forlornly from it as if, below Luc's grasp, my arm was dead. I couldn't recall how I had always managed, walking with Bertrand. Later on, Luc and Françoise took us to a fashionable dressmaker's and bought me a russet cloth coat. I was so overcome that I could neither thank them nor turn it down. Already something moved very fast when Luc was around. Then time suddenly came back, like a shot, and once more there were minutes, hours and cigarettes. Bertrand was furious about my taking the coat. When we had left them he made a violent scene.

"Absolutely fantastic! You'd take anything from anybody, without turning a hair!"

"This isn't just anybody, it's your uncle," I replied insincerely. "Anyhow, I couldn't afford to buy the coat myself; it's horribly expensive."

"You could have done without it, couldn't you?"

In the last couple of hours I had become quite used to the beautifully fitting coat, and this last sentence shocked me. There was a certain kind of logic which Bertrand couldn't follow. I told him so, and we had a quarrel. Finally, he took me home with him, not stopping for dinner, as if he were leading me to punishment. A punishment which I knew perfectly well was to him the most intense and meaningful moment of the day. As we lay side by side, he kissed me with a sort of trembling deference that I found touching and frightening at the same time. I much preferred the careless gaiety and young, animal quality of our first embraces. But when he lay with his body on mine, seeking me impatiently, I forgot everything but him and our simultaneous whisper. This was Bertrand, this anguish, this pleasure. Even now, particularly now, this oblivious happiness of our bodies seems to me an incredible gift. But what a mocking one, when I stop to think of reason, feeling, and all the really important things in life.

Chapter 3

W E had other lunches and dinners, just the four of us or else with other friends of Luc along. Then Françoise went to spend ten days with some friends. I had come to like her immensely. She was most attentive to other people and extremely kind. Her kindness was self-assured, and yet at times she showed a fear of failing to understand, which I found particularly touching. She was earthy and comforting, with occasionally something childlike about her. She and Luc laughed a great deal together.

We went to see her off at the Gare de Lyon. I felt less shy than at first, almost relaxed and quite gay. The boredom, to which I had previously been unwilling to admit, had gone away, and I had changed for the better. I was lively and sometimes amusing, and I felt as if this state of things could go on forever. I had become accustomed to Luc's face, and when, every now and then, he gave me a sudden thrill, I told myself it was for impersonally artistic reasons, or just because I had vaguely affectionate feelings toward him.

Françoise was smiling at us from the train window. "Take care of him for me," she said as the train started to pull out of the station.

On our way back, Bertrand stopped to buy some politico-literary paper that would provide him with grounds for indignation. Luc turned to me and said hastily:

"Shall we have dinner together tomorrow?"

I was about to answer: "All right, I'll ask Bertrand," but before I could speak he added: "I'll ring you up about it." Then, as Bertrand came toward us, he asked him: "What paper did you buy?"

"I couldn't find the one I wanted," said Bertrand. ". . . Look here, Dominique, we have a class, and I think we'd better hurry."

He had taken my arm and was holding me tight, while he and Luc looked suspiciously at each other. I stood there, sheepishly. Now that Françoise was gone, everything was troubled and unpleasant. This first sign of Luc's interest was to leave a bad taste in my mouth. Up to this point I had refused to see the situation in its true light. Now, all of a sudden, I wanted to have Françoise near by, as a means of protection. I realized that our elaborately built-up foursome was only a hoax. And I was scared. Like all facile liars, I was sensitive to the atmosphere around me and had to put sincerity into the role I was playing.

"I'll take you to the Sorbonne," said Luc casually.

He had a fast, open car and drove well. We said nothing during the ride and no more than: "See you soon," when we parted company. A moment later, as Bertrand and I walked to the classroom, Bertrand observed:

"All things considered, Françoise's departure is something of a relief. We can't go on always seeing the same people."

This remark eliminated Luc from our future plans, but I had learned to be careful and didn't call the fact to his attention.

"And besides," Bertrand continued, "they're a bit old, don't you agree?"

I made no reply, and we went on in to Brême's lecture on the ethics of Epicurus. I listened somewhat distractedly. . . . Luc wanted to have dinner with me alone. It must be that happiness was within my grasp. Spreading my fingers over the wooden bench, I felt a small, irrepressible smile twist my mouth, and I turned my head so that Bertrand should not see. It lasted no more than a minute, and then I said to myself: "You're flattered; that's only natural." Burning bridges, barring all roads of escape, never letting myself be taken in by my own illusions . . . I still had all the healthy reactions of youth.

*   *   *

The next day I decided that my dinner with Luc should be amusing and inconsequential. I imagined him appearing suddenly, in a state of great excitement, and declaring his passion on the spot. Instead, he arrived late and absent-minded. I wished with all my heart that he would show some emotion over our impromptu tête-à-tête, but he did nothing of the sort and talked calmly on various subjects, with an ease which I finally came to share. He was probably the first person to put me at my ease completely. He suggested that we go to a place where we could dance while we dined and took me to Sonny's. There he ran into some friends who came and sat at our table. I thought what a vain little fool I was to have fancied, even for a moment, that he wanted to be alone with me.

Looking at the other women in the group, I realized that I lacked both style and glamor. By the time midnight came around, the siren I had all day imagined myself to be was a limp rag, ashamed of her looks and mentally calling for Bertrand, in whose eyes she was beautiful.

Luc's friends talked about Alka-Seltzer and what a boon it was for the morning after. So there was a whole category of people who took Alka-Seltzer, who treated their bodies like toys, slightly worn by the process of play, but enthusiastically patched up the next morning. Perhaps I should give up books, conversation and long walks, and go in for the pleasures of money and futility, which seemed to be so very absorbing. The point was to have the means to become a thing of beauty. Would Luc approve?

He turned to me, smiling, and asked me to dance. He took me in his arms and gently settled me there, with my head against his chin. As we danced I was conscious of his body against mine.

"Those people bore you, don't they?" he asked. "The women have a genius for chatter."

"I've never been to a real night club before," I said. "I'm dazzled."

He broke into laughter.

"You're a funny one, Dominique. I find you quite delightful. Let's go somewhere else. Come along."

After we had left Sonny's, Luc took me to a bar on the Rue Marbeuf, where we began drinking steadily. Aside from my taste for whisky, I knew it was the only thing that could loosen my tongue. Soon Luc had lost all his terror for me and seemed to me an agreeable, highly attractive man. I even felt a sort of detached tenderness for him.

We came, quite naturally, to talk about love. He said that it was a good thing, less important than people claimed, but that to love and to be loved were essential to being happy. I nodded approval. Then he went on to say that he was happy, himself, because he loved Françoise and she loved him in return. I congratulated him and said that I was not surprised, that he and Françoise were wonderful people. I sank into a melting mood.

"However," Luc said, "it would give me a great kick to have an affair with you."

I laughed foolishly, without any deep feeling.

"What about Françoise?" I asked.

"Maybe I'll tell her. She's very fond of you."

"That's just it," I said. "And then, oh, I don't know,

but you can't say such things in that offhand manner. . . ."

I was indignant, exhausted by seesawing from one situation to another. It seemed to me both entirely natural and entirely improper that Luc should offer me his bed.

"I don't know how it happens," Luc said seriously, "but there *is* something, I mean something we have in common. Lord knows I don't usually care for young girls. But we're the same type. That's not so stupid, nor so commonplace, either. In fact, it's exceedingly rare. . . . Anyhow, you can think it over."

"That's it," I said. "I'll think it over."

I must have been a pitiful sight, for Luc leaned over and kissed my cheek.

"My poor darling," he said. "I'm sorry for you. If you had any morals . . . But you haven't, any more than I. You're nice, though. You're fond of Françoise, and you're less bored with me than with Bertrand. You're in a pretty fix, I tell you!"

He burst out laughing, and I was annoyed. Later on, I always got hurt when Luc started, as he said, to sum up a given situation. This time I let my feelings show.

"It doesn't matter," he said. "In this kind of thing nothing matters too much. I like you. I love you. We'll have fun together. Nothing more than fun."

"I despise you," I answered.

I had taken on a sepulchral tone of voice, and we began to laugh together. There seemed to me something suspect about a complicity that had been set up so fast.

"Now I'm taking you home," said Luc. "It's late. Or, if you like, we can watch the sunrise from the Quai de Bercy."

We drove to the Quai de Bercy, and Luc stopped the car. The sky was white above the Seine, and the great cranes, which had not yet begun to work, were like so many inanimate toys. The sky was white and also gray, as it rose, with its usual deliberate obstinacy, over the sleeping houses, the bridges and other ironwork, to meet the day. Luc sat perfectly still beside me, puffing at a cigarette. I held out my hand, he took it in his and we drove slowly to my boardinghouse. In front of the door, he let go my hand, I stepped out of the car and we exchanged smiles. I tumbled into bed, thinking that I really ought to take off my clothes, wash my stockings and put my dress on a hanger. Instead, I fell sound asleep.

Chapter 4

I WOKE up with the painful awareness of a problem requiring solution. What Luc had proposed was a game, a most alluring game. But it threatened to undermine the fairly solid feelings I had toward Bertrand and also something within myself, something which dimly but violently opposed any strictly temporary commitment such as Luc had suggested. I was willing to admit that no passion, no liaison, could last for long, but not to set up this fleeting quality as an absolute law. Like everyone that lives in large part on make-believe, I had to write my own script and not merely act out one that was handed to me.

Moreover, I knew that this game—if you can call it a game when two people attract each other and see in their relationship the possibility of at least a temporary rift in their loneliness—was dangerous. I mustn't be foolhardy and go beyond my depth. The instant I was "tamed," as Françoise had put it, that is, accepted and tolerated by Luc, I should never be able to leave him without suffering. Bertrand, of course, was incapable of anything beyond loving me. I said this to myself with a feeling of tenderness for him, but all the while I let myself think of Luc without the slightest inhibition. When one is young and on the threshold of life's long deception, rashness is all. And, as a matter of fact, I had never decided anything for myself; I had always been chosen. Why not continue to let myself be led? There would be Luc's charm, the boredom of everyday life, the long evenings. . . . Everything would follow its natural course; it was no use trying to figure out exactly how it would go.

Armed with this smugly fatalistic attitude, I continued to attend classes. I met Bertrand and our common friends, and we had lunch together on the Rue Cujas. Yet this daily routine seemed quite abnormal to me. All the while I belonged with Luc. I felt this dimly while Bertrand's friend, Jean-Jacques, made sarcastic remarks about my dreamy condition.

"Really, Dominique, you must be in love. Bertrand, what have you done to make this girl so absent-minded?"

"I don't know," said Bertrand.

I looked at him and saw that he had turned red and was avoiding my glance. It was really incredible that my accomplice and companion of a whole year should turn into an enemy. I had an impulsive urge to say: "Bertrand, believe me, you mustn't suffer. It's all too bad, and I don't really like it." I might even have gone so far as to add, stupidly: "Remember those summer days, those winter days we spent in your room. . . . All that can't be wiped out in three weeks; it doesn't make sense." I should have liked him to agree violently with what I said, to comfort me and take me back. Because he loved me, I knew that. But he wasn't a man. In some men, and especially in Luc, there was a vigor far beyond that of any of these boys. Not that I knew it from experience. . . .

"Stop bothering Dominique," said Catherine, with her usual bossy air. "Come along, Dominique; men are brutes. Let's go have a cup of coffee together."

Once we were outside, she explained that none of this was important, that Bertrand was devoted to me and I shouldn't worry about such sudden changes of humor. I didn't dream of contradicting her. There was no reason why Bertrand should be humiliated in front of our friends. Actually, I was fed up with all their talk of boys and girls, their little tragedies and the childishness of their so-called amorous nonsense. Only Bertrand and his suffering were real, and no subject for trifling. Everything moved so fast! I had scarcely begun to neglect Bertrand, and there they were, discussing, explaining and driving me, through sheer irritation, to precipitate matters and lend significance to what might have been no more than a passing aberration.

"You've got it all wrong," I said to Catherine. "I'm not thinking about Bertrand."

"Ah!" she exclaimed.

I read in her face such ghoulish curiosity and such a mania for giving advice that I couldn't help laughing.

"I'm thinking of taking the veil," I said solemnly.

Without evincing the least surprise, Catherine launched into a long peroration about the joys of life, the sun, the tiny birds . . . "all those things which sheer madness is impelling you to leave behind! . . ." She even talked about sexual pleasure, lowering her voice to say: "It's no use refusing to look things in the face. . . . *That* means quite a lot, after all. . . ." If I had really been serious about it, her description of the sensual side of life would have thrown me into the arms of religion. Could "that" possibly be anyone's idea of life? After all, if I was bored, I was bored passionately. And Catherine abounded in commonplaces; she verged so disgustingly on the intimate confidences that one streetwalker might make to another that without the slightest compunction I walked off and left her. "So much for Catherine and all her devotion!" I thought gaily to myself. And I sang under my breath, in a positively ferocious manner.

I strolled about for an hour, walked into half a dozen shops and passed the time of day with everyone I met. Paris was mine! Paris belonged to the unscrupulous, the unconcerned; this was something of which I had always been painfully aware, because I had not been among them. Now, at last, it belonged to me as well. This was my sharp-edged, hard-boiled, golden city. I was carried away by something that might have been joy. I walked fast, chafing under my own impatience and the heat of the blood that pulsed through my veins, and feeling quite ridiculously young. In such a moment of wild happiness I felt that I had grasped a truth much more significant than all the miserable truisms to which I clung when I was sad.

I went into a moving-picture house on the Champs-Elysées, which specialized in old films. A young man came and sat beside me, and I saw at a glance that he was attractive, in spite of the fact that I don't care for blond hair. Soon he moved his elbow against mine and extended a cautious hand in the direction of my knee. I seized his hand in mid-air and held it tight, wanting all the time to giggle. My customary scorn for the vulgar promiscuity and furtive embraces of a darkened theater had melted away. I was holding a strange young man's warm hand, and although he didn't in the least interest me, I felt like giggling and having some fun. He rubbed his captive hand against mine and slowly advanced one knee. I watched him with curiosity and fear, which added up to tacit encouragement. I was afraid, and he was, too, that from one moment to the next I might go proper on him, and like an indignant old maid get up and go away. My heart was beating faster than usual; was it emotion or the film? Because the film was good and actually held my attention. There ought to be special showings of dull films for people whose real interest is a pickup. The young man turned a questioning face to mine; the film was Swedish with backgrounds which projected some of their light from the screen, so I could see that he was, as I had suspected, a handsome enough fellow. "Handsome, but not my type," I said to myself as he brought a wary face closer to mine. For a second I thought of the people directly behind us, who must be thinking . . . He kissed well, but at the same time he increased the pressure of his knee and once more stretched out his hand, in a sly, clumsy attempt to follow up the advantage which I had unresistingly allowed him to obtain. Brusquely, I got up and went out, no doubt leaving him flabbergasted behind me.

I emerged on the Champs-Elysées with the taste of a strange mouth on mine, and decided to go home and read a new book.

It was a good novel by Sartre, *L'Age de Raison*, and I plunged into it blissfully. I was young, attracted by one man and loved by another. I had a stupid little girlish conflict to solve and I was rapidly acquiring importance. A married man, another woman . . . in short a foursome, scheduled to be played in Paris in the spring. I made it into a neat equation, one as cynical as you could hope to find. What's more, I felt quite smug about it. I accepted all the sorrows and conflicts and pleasures that were to come. I accepted them in advance and laughed them off with scorn.

I read until night fell. I laid down my book, rested my head on my arm and watched the sky change from mauve to gray. Suddenly I felt weak and defenseless. My life was going by, and I was doing nothing but jeer. Oh, to have a cheek against mine, to have someone for keeps and press him to me with all the shattering violence of love! I wasn't so cynical as to envy Bertrand, but I was quite sad enough to appreciate the good luck of anyone who was happily in love, or fresh from a desperate encounter, or in bondage of any description.

Chapter 5

DURING the next two weeks I went out with Luc several times, but there were always friends of his along. They were mainly globe-trotters of engaging appearance and with stories to tell. Luc talked quickly and amusingly, looked at me with indulgence and maintained the hurried, absent air which made me doubt that I really interested him. Afterward, he drove me home, got out of the car and kissed me lightly on the cheek before going on. He made no further reference to the affair which he had half proposed before, and I felt both relieved and disappointed. Finally he said that Françoise was coming home two days later, and I realized that the time since her departure had gone by like a dream and I had been talking to myself about absolutely nothing.

We went to meet Françoise at the station, but without Bertrand, who for the last ten days had been avoiding me. I missed him but took advantage of my solitude to live the idle, casual life I loved so well. The knowledge that he was unhappy kept me from being too unhappy myself.

Françoise arrived, all smiles, kissed us both and said

that neither of us looked well. It would do us good to accept an invitation to spend a week end in the country, which she had just received from Luc's sister, that is, Bertrand's mother. I protested that I hadn't been asked and, besides, I wasn't on good terms with Bertrand. And Luc said that his sister got on his nerves. But Françoise had an answer for everything. Bertrand, she said, had asked his mother to invite me, "probably for the express purpose of clearing up this misunderstanding." And as for Luc, every now and then he really ought to show some family feeling.

She smiled at me, and I smiled back, bending over backward to make myself agreeable. She had put on weight and was a little too heavy, but was so warmhearted and trusting that I was glad nothing had happened between Luc and myself and we could go on being happy, all three of us together, the way we had been before. I'd go back to Bertrand; I didn't really find him so boring; and he was terribly intelligent. Yes, Luc and I had been very wise. But as I sat down in the car, between him and Françoise, I looked at him for a second as if he were someone I had given up, and it gave me a strangely disagreeable little shock inside.

*   *   *

We left Paris on a beautiful afternoon to go to the house of Bertrand's mother. I knew that her husband had left her a very pretty country place and the fact that I was going somewhere for the week end gave me something to talk about in snobbish terms which I had never had a chance to use before. Bertrand had informed me that his mother was an extremely agreeable person. He said this in the studiedly careless manner in which young people like to speak of their parents, as if to imply that of course they are quite independent of them. I had gone to the expense of some linen slacks, because Catherine's were really too large for me. This purchase made a hole in my budget, but I knew that Luc and Françoise would come to the rescue if I really needed anything. The ease with which I mentally agreed to this surprised me, but like most people who live on the best possible terms with themselves, at least in small things, I attributed this ease to their kindness rather than to my own indiscretion. Anyhow, it is healthier to see the good points of others than to analyze our own bad ones.

Luc and Françoise picked us up at a café on the Boulevard Saint-Michel. He still seemed tired and a little sad, and once we reached the highway he drove almost dangerously fast. Bertrand broke into a gale of nervous laughter and I joined him. Françoise looked around with the disconcerted expression peculiar to people who are far too kind to raise a row, even if their lives depend upon it.

"What makes you laugh?" she asked.

"They're young," said Luc. "At twenty years of age, one still goes in for fits of uncontrollable laughter."

For some reason this remark rubbed me the wrong way. I didn't want Luc to treat Bertrand and me like a couple, still less like a couple of children.

"We're laughing because we're nervous," I said. "Because you're driving too fast and it makes us feel very small."

"You must come out with me, some day, my pet," said Luc, "and I'll teach you how to drive."

This was the first time Luc had ever called me by an endearing name in public. "Maybe that's what's called a break," I thought, as Françoise shot her husband a quick look. Then such an idea seemed to me utterly ridiculous. I didn't believe in telltale blunders, intercepted glances and lightning-swift intuitions. One sentence that is a great favorite with novelists never fails to surprise me: "Suddenly she knew he was lying to her."

We were almost there. Luc turned sharply into a narrow road and I was thrown against Bertrand, who held me firmly and tenderly in his arms in a most embarrassing fashion. I couldn't bear for Luc to see me in this posture. It seemed to me unnecessarily vulgar and indelicate.

"You look like a bird," said Françoise, who had turned around to see how we were faring.

Her face was really kind, and there was something tactfully restrained in her manner. She did not feel called upon to display the conniving approval which middle-aged women so often bestow upon adolescent couples. She merely seemed to think that I looked comfortable in Bertrand's arms and that there was something touching about me. I was happy enough to look touching, for it relieved me of the necessity to think, believe or even reply.

"An old bird," I said. "I feel old."

"So do I," said Françoise, "but that's slightly more natural."

Luc turned his head toward her, with a faint smile. I thought suddenly: "They're attractive to each other. They still go to bed together, I know it. Luc sleeps right up against her, in the same bed, and makes love to her. . . . Does he think of Bertrand's body and mine in the same way? Does he imagine them together? And is he vaguely jealous of me, as I am of him?"

"Here we are," exclaimed Bertrand. "I see another car, which means that Mother has some of her usual guests."

"In that case, we shan't stay," said Luc. "I have a perfect horror of my dear sister's guests, and I know a very pleasant inn close by."

"Now, now," said Françoise. "Don't be so difficult. The house is lovely, and Dominique has never seen it. Come, Dominique. . . ."

Taking me by the hand she led me across the lawn and up to the house. I followed her, thinking all the while that I had very nearly played the mean trick of causing her husband to be unfaithful to her, and that I liked her so very much that I'd go to any length to avoid causing her pain. But obviously she would never have known the difference.

"Here you are, at last!" said a shrill voice.

Bertrand's mother burst from a hedge. I had never seen her before. She looked at me searchingly, the way a young man's mother looks at any girl he brings for the first time to the house. My immediate impression was that she was blond and a little loud. She circled around us, chirping in a somewhat nerve-wracking manner. Luc stared at her as if she were a calamity, while Bertrand seemed slightly embarrassed, all of which inspired me to be on my best behavior. It was with a feeling of relief that I found myself in my room. The bed was very high, with coarse sheets, like those of my childhood. I opened my window onto rustling green trees, and a strong odor of moist earth and grass filled the room.

"Do you like it?" asked Bertrand, with a half pleased, half abashed air.

I realized that this week end with me in his mother's house must be meaningful to him, and I said with a smile: "You have a very lovely house. As to your mother, I don't know her yet, but she seems very kind."

"So you don't mind being here. . . . Anyhow, my room is next door."

His laugh held a hint of complicity. I liked strange houses, black-and-white-tiled bathrooms and imperious young men. He took me into his arms and gently kissed my lips. I knew the smell of his breath and his way of kissing. I had never told him about the young man at the movies. He would have taken it badly. By this time I took it badly myself. Seen in its true perspective, the episode was rather shameful, comic if you like, and yet vaguely disturbing. For the space of one afternoon, I had been lighthearted and free; I was so no longer.

"Come on down to dinner," I said to Bertrand, as he bent over to kiss me again, his eyes slightly dilated. I liked to feel his desire. On the other hand, I didn't like myself. That type of wild, cold little girl—"I have white teeth and a black heart"—seemed to me play-acting for old gentlemen.

The dinner was deadly. Sure enough, there were friends of Bertrand's mother: a garrulous couple, very much in the social swim. At dessert, Richard, the husband, chairman of some board of directors, could not resist harping on the usual theme:

"What about you, young lady? Are you one of those wretched existentialists? . . . As a matter of fact, my dear Marthe"—he had turned now to Bertrand's mother—"these disillusioned young people are beyond me. At their age, hang it all, we loved life. When I was young, we enjoyed ourselves, we kicked up our heels, but it was all good, clean fun!"

His wife and Bertrand's mother laughed knowingly, Luc yawned, while Bertrand readied a speech to which no one would pay any attention. With her usual good will, Françoise was trying to understand what made these people so boring. This was about the tenth time that pink-cheeked, gray-haired gentlemen had put on the "good, clean fun" act for my benefit, chewing their food all the more gleefully for not having the slightest idea of the meaning of the word "existentialism." I made no reply.

"My dear Richard," said Luc, "I'm afraid that it's only at your age—our age, I mean—that we can afford to kick up our heels. These young people make love, which is quite all right, too. You need an office and a secretary if you're to have good, clean fun."

The fun-loving Richard had nothing more to say, and the rest of the dinner went off without commotion. Everyone but Luc and myself talked, after a fashion. Luc was the only other one to be as violently bored as I was, and I wondered if this intolerance of boredom was not the first sign of partnership between us.

After dinner, since the weather was mild, we went out on the terrace. Bertrand was sent to get some whisky and Luc told me in a whisper that I mustn't drink too much.

"I can hold it; I know how to behave," I said with annoyance.

"It would make me jealous," he said. "I like you to be fuzzy and talk nonsense, only not with anyone but me."

"And what am I to do the rest of the time?"

"Pull a long face, the way you did at dinner."

"What about your own face? Do you imagine you looked gay? In spite of what you said, I don't believe you belong to the pink-cheeked, fun-loving generation."

He laughed.

"Come have a walk in the garden."

"In the dark? What about Bertrand and the others?"

I was in a panic.

"They've bored us long enough. Come along."

He took me by the arm and glanced at our fellow guests. Bertrand had not yet returned with the whisky. I thought vaguely that when he did return he would look for us in the garden, catch up with us under a tree and perhaps kill Luc, the way it happened in *Pelléas and Mélisande.*

"I'm taking this young woman for a sentimental walk," Luc said, addressing the company from a safe distance.

Without looking around, I heard Françoise's laughter. He led me down a gravel path, light at the beginning, but soon melting into the dark. Suddenly I was afraid. I wanted to be with my parents, on the banks of the Yonne River.

"I'm scared," I said to Luc.

He did not laugh but took my hand. I wished he could always be just the way he was then, silent, grave, protecting and tender, that he would never go away, that he would say he loved me and take me in his arms. He stopped and did take me in his arms. I leaned against his jacket and closed my eyes. All these last days had been no more than a vain flight from this moment, from the hands that were tilting my face and the soft, warm mouth that was so well suited to mine. He kept his fingers around my face and tightened his grip as we kissed. I put my arms around his neck, feeling frightened of myself, of him, of everything that was not this moment.

Right away I liked his mouth. He kissed me without

saying a word, occasionally raising his head to take a breath. I could see his face above mine, in the semi-darkness, at the same time absent and concentrated, like a mask. Then slowly he returned to me. Soon I could no longer distinguish his features, and closed my eyes, while my temples, my eyelids, my breast were all flooded with heat. I had an absolutely new feeling which had none of the haste or impatience of desire, but was happy and deliberate and disturbing.

Luc broke away from me, and I stumbled slightly. He took me by the arm and, without a word, we walked back through the garden. I was thinking that I should be content to kiss him until the break of day. Bertrand ran out of kisses too soon; desire made them superfluous in his eyes. They were only a stage on the road to pleasure, not something inexhaustible and self-sufficient, as Luc had revealed them to me.

"Your garden is magnificent," Luc said now, smiling at his sister. "Unfortunately, it's a bit late."

"It's never too late," said Bertrand dryly.

He stared at me, and I turned away my eyes. I wanted to be alone in the darkness of my room, in order to remember and understand those moments in the garden. I must set them aside during the rest of the general conversation, from which I'd be secretly withdrawn. Then later, I could pick them up again in my room. I would lie flat on my bed, with open eyes, turning their memory over and over in order either to destroy it or to let it become part of me forever. I closed my door that night, and Bertrand did not knock.

Chapter 6

THE next morning went slowly by. I woke up to an atmosphere of peaceful repose that took me back to my childhood. But what lay ahead was not a long, lonely, yellow-leaved day, interspersed with reading. It was the necessity of facing "the others," in whose midst I had a part to play. At first, the prospect of taking on this responsibility was more than I could bear, and with a feeling of physical discomfort I burrowed into my pillow. Then I remembered last night and Luc's kisses, and something inside me was torn gently asunder.

The bathroom was wonderful. Once in my bath I began to sing, under my breath, to a jazz tune: "I've got to do something about it, abooouuut it . . ." There was a loud bang on the wall.

"Can't respectable people be allowed to sleep?"

It was a joyful voice, Luc's voice. If I had been born ten years earlier, before Françoise, we should have lived together and he would have laughingly stopped me from singing in my morning bath; we should have waked up in the same bed and enjoyed a lifetime of happiness, instead of finding ourselves in this blind alley. It *was* a blind alley, and perhaps that was why we hesitated to enter it, in spite of our show of bravado. I must escape from him, go away. I got out of my bath and found a fluffy bathrobe that smelled of an old country closet. As I slipped into it, I came around to the sensible conclusion that I should let things take their course. I should not pursue my analytical dissection but wait calmly and bravely for whatever might come. I positively purred with insincerity over the virtue of this decision.

I put on my new linen slacks and looked at myself in the mirror. I didn't care for what it showed me: un-combed hair, an angular face and a "nice" expression. I should have preferred regular features, coils of braided hair, a severe but carnal face, the somber eyes of a girl destined to make men suffer. Of course, if I threw my head back I might achieve a more voluptuous air, but then any woman could do the same thing. And these slacks were ridiculous; they made me look like a match-stick. I simply couldn't go downstairs. How well I knew this form of despair! When I got off on the wrong foot with my reflection in the mirror, I was capable of sulking all day long.

But Françoise came in and set everything right.

"Why, little Dominique, you look charming! You're even younger and livelier than ever! You're a living reproach to me!"

"Why a reproach?"

Without looking up, she answered:

"I eat too many sweets, for no other reason than the fact that I'm crazy about them. And then, just look at these wrinkles. . . ."

She had some heavy lines at the corners of her eyes, and I touched them with my forefinger.

"I like them," I said. "Think of all the nights, all the exotic countries, all the strange faces that went into their imprinting. They suit you; they make you come alive. I don't know what it is, but, as I say, I like them; they have feeling and expression. I hate smooth faces."

She burst out laughing: "So you'd put beauty parlors out of business, just in order to cheer me up, would you? You're a sweet child, Dominique, very, very sweet."

"I'm not as sweet as all that," I said, feeling somewhat ashamed.

"Did I say the wrong thing? Young people have a horror of being sweet, I know. But you never make unjust or unkind remarks. And you like people. As far as I can see, you're about perfect."

"I'm not, though."

I hadn't talked about myself for a long time, although up until the time I was seventeen it was one of my favorite occupations. Now the subject was wearisome. I couldn't be interested in myself, love myself, unless Luc loved me and was interested in me. This last idea was silly.

"That's going too far," I thought aloud.

"And you're incredibly absent-minded," added Françoise.

"That's because I'm not in love."

She looked at me and I was strongly tempted to say: "Françoise, I could easily fall for Luc, and I'm very fond of you, too, so please take him away."

But Françoise broke in to say: "What about Bertrand? Is it all over?"

I shrugged my shoulders. "I no longer see him. I mean, I don't look at him any more."

"Perhaps you ought to tell him."

I made no reply. What could I say to Bertrand?—"I don't want to go on seeing you"? But I did want to see him. He meant a great deal to me.

Françoise smiled. "I understand. It's never easy. . . . Come on down to breakfast. By the way, I saw a sweater on the Rue Caumartin that would go beautifully with those slacks. We must go look at it together. . . ."

We talked gaily about clothes as we went down the stairs. The subject didn't really thrill me, but it amused me to chatter about something inconsequential, to put in an adjective here and there, to get it all wrong, make her angry and then have a good laugh. Luc and Bertrand were having breakfast together. They said something about going for a swim.

"We can go to the pool."

Bertrand was speaking. He must have thought that he'd cut a better figure than Luc in the open. Or perhaps his motive wasn't really so petty.

"Good. And I'll give Dominique a driving lesson on the way."

"Don't do anything too crazy!" exclaimed Bertrand's mother, as she came, clad in an elaborate dressing gown, into the room. "Did you sleep well? . . . And how about you, precious boy?"

Bertrand looked embarrassed. He had a solemn air which was most unbecoming. I wanted him to be gay. We always want someone we've treated badly to be gay. It's less upsetting.

Luc got up. Obviously, he couldn't bear his sister's presence. This amused me. I had physical aversions of the same kind, but I felt I must conceal them. There was something childlike in Luc's composition.

"I'm going up to get my trunks," he said.

There was a great bustle while we all looked for our swimming things. Finally everyone was ready. Bertrand went off with his mother in her guests' car, leaving Françoise, Luc and me together.

"You take the wheel," Luc said to me.

My notions of driving were rather vague, but it went off fairly well. Luc sat beside me, while from the back seat Françoise chattered on, oblivious of danger. Once more I was nostalgic for what might have been: long trips with Luc at my side, roads swept by the headlights, myself leaning against Luc's shoulders while his steady hand was on the wheel. The sun rising over the countryside and setting over the sea. . . .

"Do you know that I've never seen the sea?" I said.

There was an outburst of surprise.

"I'll show it to you one day," said Luc gently. And he shot me a smile that seemed to contain a promise. Françoise had not heard him, and she went on:

"We must take her with us, Luc, next time we go. She'll probably say: 'My, what a lot of water!'—as someone once put it, I can't remember who. . . ."

"I'll probably begin by plunging in," I said, "and talk about it later."

"It's really wonderful, you know," said Françoise. "Yellow beaches, red rocks and all that blue water rushing at them."

"I love your description," said Luc with a laugh. "Yellow, red, blue . . . just what a schoolgirl would say . . . a very young schoolgirl," he added apologetically, turning toward me. "Some older schoolgirls are very bright indeed. . . . Turn left, Dominique, if you can."

I could. A moment later we reached a green lawn, and in the middle was a large pool filled with light blue water, which froze me at sight. Soon we were standing, in our bathing suits, at the edge of the pool. I had met Luc as he came out of his cabin, and he seemed unhappy. I asked him why and he said with a diffident smile:

"I don't find myself very good-looking."

He wasn't, either. He was gaunt, stooping, and white-skinned. But he looked so miserable, holding his towel in front of him, like an awkward adolescent boy, that I felt sorry for him.

"Come, come," I said blithely, "you're not as bad as all that!"

He glanced at me sideways, seeming somewhat shocked, and then burst out laughing.

"You're getting to be very disrespectful!"

Then he ran off and dove into the water. Almost at once he stuck out his head, with cries of distress, and Françoise came to sit on the edge.

"It's atrociously cold," said Luc from the pool. "It's sheer madness to bathe in May."

"The merry, merry month of May," said Bertrand's mother irrelevantly, but no sooner had she dipped her foot into the water than she went off and got dressed. I looked at the chattering white-skinned group by the pool, and a sort of mild gaiety swept over me, together with the eternally recurrent question: "What in the world am I doing here?"

"Aren't you going in?" asked Bertrand.

He stood, balancing on one foot before me, and I glanced at him approvingly. I knew that he exercised with dumbbells every morning. Once, when we had spent a week end together, he had mistaken my dozing for deep sleep and had done gymnastics in front of the open window. At the time, I had stifled a gale of laughter, but now I saw that his efforts had been worth while, for he had a trim, healthy look about him.

"We're lucky to have dark skins," he observed. "Just look at the others."

"Let's get into the water," I said, fearful lest he make some critical remark about his mother.

I eased myself reluctantly in but felt honor bound to swim once around the pool. I came out shivering, and Françoise rubbed me down with a towel. I wondered why she had never had a child. With her wide hips, full-blown body and kindly ways, she was cut out to be a mother. It was really a shame.

Chapter 7

TWO days after this week end, I had an appointment with Luc at six o'clock. I felt that any further trifling would put something suffocating and irreparable between us. Like a young girl of the seventeenth century, I was prepared to ask an indemnity for his kiss. We were to meet at a bar on the Quai Voltaire. To my surprise, Luc was already there, looking tired and unwell. I sat down beside him and he ordered two whiskies. Then he asked for news of Bertrand.

"He's all right."

"Is he very upset?" he asked without a trace of mockery in his voice.

"Why should he be upset?" I asked stupidly.

"He's no fool."

"I don't see why you have to talk about Bertrand. He's really . . ."

"Quite unimportant?"

This time he was ironical, and I reacted impatiently.

"He's not unimportant, but there's no use taking him too seriously. If we're going to discuss serious matters, what about Françoise?"

He laughed.

"You'll see what a funny business this is. For some reason, the . . . well, let's say the other person's partner seems more of an obstacle than your own. Horrible as it may sound, when you know someone well, you know his or her manner of suffering, and it seems endurable to you. No, perhaps not endurable, but the fact that you know it makes it less terrifying."

"I don't know much about Bertrand's suffering," I said.

"You haven't had time. I've been married ten years, so I've had plenty of occasions to see Françoise suffer. It's most unpleasant."

We were quiet for a moment. Probably both of us were picturing the sufferings of Françoise. I imagined her with her face turned to the wall.

"It's absurd," said Luc at last. "But you see, it isn't as I thought."

He picked up the glass, tilted his head back and drank down the contents in a single swallow. I felt as if I were watching a movie. I told myself that this was not the time to be cool and detached, but I had an impression that the whole thing was totally unreal. Luc was there, he would decide what was to be done, and that made everything all right. He bent forward a little, twirling the empty glass rhythmically in his hands. He did not look at me as he spoke.

"Of course, I've had other affairs. Most of the time Françoise knew nothing about them. Except for a few unfortunate instances. It was never very serious." He straightened up, almost angrily, and went on: "It's not very serious with you, either. Nothing is very serious. Nothing really matters except Françoise."

I don't know why, but I listened to him without distress, as if I were visiting a philosophy class with which I had no real connection.

"This is different, all the same. At first I wanted you the way a man of my sort wants a kittenish, hard-to-get little girl. That's what I told you. I wanted to tame you, to have you for a night. I never thought . . ."

He turned toward me, took my hands and continued in a much gentler fashion. I looked at his face from near by, studying its every line and listening with passionate interest to what he had to say. At last I felt like giving someone my wholehearted attention; I was delivered from myself and the still, small voice within.

"I never thought that I should come to have such a high opinion of you. I have, though, Dominique, and I love you, besides. I'll never love you 'for keeps,' as children say, but you and I are alike, somehow. I don't want just to sleep with you, I want us to live together, to share a holiday. We'd be very happy, very tender; I'd introduce you to the sea, to money and the freedom it brings. We'd be much less bored. There you have it."

"I like the idea very well," I said.

"Of course, I'd go back to Françoise. But what risk do you run? The risk of getting attached to me and letting yourself in for some pain? That's better than boredom, any day, isn't it? You'd rather be first happy and then unhappy than stay bored, wouldn't you?"

"Of course," I echoed.

"So what risk do you run?" Luc repeated, as if to convince himself of the point he was making.

"Never mind about the pain," I said. "Don't let's make too much of that. My heart isn't that fragile."

"Good," said Luc. "We'll think it over. Let's talk about something else. Will you have another drink?"

We drank our respective healths. What stood out most clearly in my mind was that we were very likely going off together in a car, in just the way that I had wildly imagined while believing that it could never come true. I should manage, somehow, not to get too attached to him, knowing that all my bridges had been burned in advance. After all, I wasn't completely crazy.

We went out and walked along the quays. Luc laughed and talked with me, and I laughed back. I told myself that with him there must always be laughter; certainly it reflected my present mood. "Laughter goes naturally with love," as Alain puts it. But in this case, it was a question not of love but of an understanding. And, finally, I felt rather proud: I was in Luc's thoughts; he had a high opinion of me and desired me. My piddling conscience, which always reflected such a very poor image of me, might be a little too severe and pessimistic, after all.

After leaving Luc, I went into another bar and spent the four hundred francs which should have gone for my dinner on a third glass of whisky. Within ten minutes I felt wonderfully well: I was tender, kind and attractive and I must find someone who might benefit from my explanation of all the hard, sweet and sharp things I knew about life. I could have talked for hours, but the barman was uninteresting. So I went to a café on the Rue Saint-Jacques, where I ran into Bertrand, who was sitting alone with a stack of coasters from the drinks he had consumed before him. I sat down, and he seemed delighted to see me.

"I was just thinking of you. There's a new be-bop orchestra at the Kentucky. Shall we go? We haven't danced for ages."

"I haven't a sou," I said dolefully.

"My mother gave me ten thousand francs the other day. We'll have a few drinks and then we'll go."

"But it's only eight o'clock," I objected, "and it doesn't open before ten."

"We'll have a lot of drinks, then," said Bertrand gaily.

I was delighted. We always had a good time dancing to be-bop music together, and already a juke box was making my legs fidgety. When Bertrand paid for the drinks, I saw that he had had plenty. He was extremely gay. Besides, he was my best friend, my brother, and I loved him very deeply. We made the rounds of five or six bars until ten o'clock and ended up beautifully drunk and gay but not at all sentimental. When we got to the Kentucky, the orchestra had already begun to play, but there were very few people, and we had the floor almost to ourselves. Contrary to my expectations, we relaxed and danced very well. More than anything else I loved the music, the impulse it gave me and the pleasure felt by my own body. We sat down only long enough to drink.

"Jazz music," I observed confidentially to Bertrand, "is a form of accelerated unconcern."

He sat up abruptly.

"That's it, exactly. Very interesting. A top-notch definition. Good for you, Dominique."

"You see!"

"The whisky is terrible here, but the music's good. Unconcern, eh? Unconcern with what?"

"I don't know. Listen, the trumpet is not only unconcerned, it's necessary as well. It had to carry that note to the very end. Did you feel it? Necessary. It's like love, you know, physical love. There comes a time when you simply have to . . . When it can't be anyway else."

"Quite true, and very interesting. Shall we dance?"

We spent the night drinking, dancing and exchanging paradoxical definitions. At the end it was all a dizzy whirl of faces and feet, of Bertrand's arm sending me away until the music hurled me back to meet him, and the incredible warmth and suppleness of our bodies.

"They're closing up," said Bertrand. "It's four o'clock."

"My boardinghouse will be closed, too," I remarked.

"That doesn't matter."

It didn't matter at all. We were going to his room and stretch out on his bed, and it was quite natural that I should have the weight of Bertrand's body on mine, just as I had had it all winter, and that we should be happy together.

Chapter 8

I LAY close to him next morning while he slept, his hip touching mine. It was early, but I couldn't get back to sleep. I said to myself that just as he was immersed in his dreams, so my real self, too, was infinitely far away, beyond the suburban houses, the fields, the trees, the haunts of childhood, standing at the end of a garden path, in the guise of a motionless statue. The girl bending over the sleeper was only a pallid reflection of this permanent self, choosing to follow one of the lives that had opened before her, while those she had rejected were frozen, like stone birds which now could never take flight from the statue's shoulder.

I stretched, got up and put on my clothes. Bertrand opened one eye, yawned, said "Good morning," and ran one hand over his cheeks and chin, complaining of the stubble. I made an appointment with him for that evening and went to my room to study. But I couldn't concentrate. It was dreadfully hot and was now almost noon. I was to lunch with Luc and Françoise, and it hardly seemed worth while to work for the intervening hour. I went out again to buy some cigarettes, came back, started to smoke one and realized as I lit it that I had not consciously lived a single one of my acts of the morning. For hours there had been nothing in me but a vague instinct to cling to my usual routine. Nothing at all. And where could I have found anything else to which to cling? I didn't believe in the marvelous human smile to be glimpsed on the face of a fellow bus-rider, or in the palpitating life of the city streets, and I didn't love Bertrand. I needed someone or something. As I lit my cigarette, I said this, half aloud, over and over: "Someone, or something," and it had a melodramatic sound, melodramatic and funny. So, like Catherine, I had moments of sentimental exasperation. I loved love and words pertaining to love: "tender, cruel, sweet, trusting, excessive," and yet I loved no one. Luc, perhaps, when he was near, but since yesterday I hadn't dared think about him. I didn't care for the taste of renunciation that rose in my throat when his image passed before me.

I was waiting for Luc and Françoise when I was seized by a feeling of nausea and dizziness and had to run to the cloakroom. When it was gone I lifted up my head and looked at myself in the mirror. I had plenty of time to count the days. "That's it!" I said aloud to myself. The nightmare which I knew all too well for having been through it, mistakenly, many times before had come back to haunt me. But this time . . . Of course, it might be the result of last night's whisky and I had

no reason to worry. I debated furiously with myself,
looking at my reflection in the glass with a mixture of
curiosity and scorn. Trapped, that was it! I must tell
Françoise. She was the only one who could get me
out of this trouble.

But I didn't tell Françoise. I didn't have the nerve.
Luc plied us with drinks during lunch and to some extent I forgot and talked myself into looking at things
more coolly. But what if Bertrand, who was obviously
jealous of Luc, had devised this way to keep me? I
seemed to have all the symptoms. . . .

The following week brought an early summer heat
wave, of an intensity such as I had never imagined.
My room was stifling and I walked about the streets in
search of relief. I asked Catherine vague questions about
how women got out of such fixes, but I never dared
let on that I was in one myself. And I had no wish to
see Luc and Françoise, the strong and the free. I was
sick as a dog, with intervals of nervous laughter, and
had no strength to look ahead or make plans. By the
end of the week I felt sure that I was going to have a
baby, Bertrand's baby, and the certainty was actually
calming. I must do something about it. . . .

But just before examinations I found that once more
I had been mistaken; the whole thing was only another
nightmare. I sailed through my written tests in the very
best of humors. For ten days I had had only one thing
on my mind, and now the rediscovery of other people's
existence filled me with wonder. Once more, everything was possible, and gay. Françoise dropped in to

see me and was appalled by the torrid heat of my room. She suggested that I study for my orals at their house, so I went and installed myself, quite alone, on a white rug, with the blinds half drawn over the windows. Françoise would come in around five o'clock, show me her day's purchases and question me, without too much real interest, about the material my exam was supposed to cover. We ended up by joking, and Luc arrived in time to join our laughter. Then we went to have dinner at a sidewalk restaurant and they took me home. Only once that week did Luc come in before Françoise. Then he came into the room where I was working, knelt down on the book-strewn rug, took me in his arms and kissed me, without saying a word. When his lips were on mine I felt as if I had never known any others, as if for the last two weeks I had thought of nothing else. He said he would write to me during the holidays and that, if I liked, we might arrange to spend a week together. He caressed the nape of my neck and sought my mouth. I longed to lie on his shoulder until night, and perhaps to complain gently because we weren't supposed really to love each other.

The academic year was over.

PART TWO

Chapter 1

OUR house was long and gray. A meadow ran down to the sluggish, green, foam-flecked Yonne River, with swallows flying overhead and poplar trees bordering each side. There was one poplar, in particular, in whose shade I liked to lie. I lay with my feet propped up against the trunk and my head lost in the shadows of the branches, which I could see stirring in the wind, high above me. The earth smelled of warm grass and gave me a feeling of mingled impotence and joy. I knew this landscape under every kind of weather. I had known it before I ever knew Paris, the streets of Paris and the Seine, or men. And it was unchanging.

By a sheer miracle, I had passed my examinations.

I lingered to read under the tree and then strolled slowly up to the house for dinner. My younger brother had died, under tragic circumstances, fifteen years before, and this had thrown my mother into a lasting melancholia which pervaded the whole house. Within its walls, sorrow was redolent of piety. My father tiptoed about, carrying shawls for my mother.

Bertrand wrote to me—a curious, obscure letter, full of references to the last night we had spent together, after the evening at the Kentucky, a night when he claimed to have treated me without due respect. I couldn't remember any lack of respect on his part, since our physical relationship was quite simple and satisfactory, and for a long time I couldn't imagine what he meant. Finally I realized that he was trying to establish an erotic complicity between us. In his search for something to bind us together, he was clutching at straws, this time at a very low level. Instinctively, I resented his effort to complicate the happiest and most honest thing we had possessed. I did not know that there are circumstances under which even the worst is preferable to the expected and the mediocre. For Bertrand, the expected, mediocre thing was that I no longer loved him. I knew that he was hankering after "me," and not "us," since a month ago, "we" had passed out of existence. And this especially grieved me.

No news from Luc all month long, only an affectionate card from Françoise, to which he had added his signature. I told myself over and over, with a certain stupid pride, that I didn't love him, as was proved by the fact that I didn't suffer from our separation. I never stopped to think that if this indifference were to be really reassuring I should have felt humiliated by it rather than self-congratulatory. But all these subtleties annoyed me. I had myself so very well in hand.

And then I loved this house, which I should by all rights have found boring. I was bored, of course, but my boredom was pleasant and not shameful, as it would have been in Paris. I made myself agreeable to everyone, and enjoyed doing so. What a relief to wander from one piece of furniture or one field to another, to live from one day to the next without any alternative before me! To lie still and acquire a painless coat of tan, to wait without tedium for the holidays to be over. The holidays were a splotch of faded yellow.

At last came a letter from Luc. He told me he would be in Avignon on the second of September and would wait there for either my arrival or that of a letter. Immediately I decided to go there in person, and the past month seemed beatifically simple. It was just like Luc—the casual tone of the letter, the ridiculous and unexpected choice of Avignon as a meeting place.

I embarked on an ocean of lies, and wrote Catherine to send me a bogus invitation. In the same mail as her prompt response she sent me another letter, expressing surprise. Bertrand, and indeed the whole gang, had gone off in the opposite direction, so who on earth was my destination? My lack of confidence in her was positively offensive. I wrote her a note of thanks, pointing out that if she wanted to hurt Bertrand, she had only to tell him about my letter, which she proceeded to do, under the pretext that she was his friend.

On September first, I set out, with a minimum of

luggage, for Avignon. Fortunately it was on the way to the Riviera, to which I had said I was going. My parents went with me to the station, and there were incomprehensible tears in my eyes when I said good-by. It seemed to me as if for the first time I were leaving my childhood and the security of my family behind me. I was sure that I was going to dislike Avignon.

* * *

After Luc's long silence and casual letter, I had formed a rather hard, detached picture of him and arrived at Avignon very much on my guard, a singularly uncomfortable frame of mind for a supposed lovers' meeting. I was not going off with Luc because either of us loved the other, but because we spoke the same language and there was a strong attraction between us. When I came right down to it, these reasons seemed highly insufficient and the whole trip terrified me.

But once again Luc gave me a surprise. He was waiting anxiously on the platform and beamed with joy when he saw me. When I got out, he clasped me in his arms and gave me a light kiss.

"You look marvelously well. I'm glad you came."

"You, too," I said, after a look at his face. He was slim, tan and considerably more handsome than when I had last seen him, in Paris.

"There's no reason why we should stay at Avignon, you know," he reassured me. "We'll go have a look at the sea. Wasn't that our original purpose? Later, we can make up our minds what we want to do."

His car was in front of the station. He threw my bag in the back, and off we started. I felt completely dazed and, contrarily, a little disappointed. I hadn't remembered him as so attractive or so gay. The road was lovely, with plane trees on each side. Luc smoked and we drove fast, top down, into the sun. I said to myself: "Here I am; this is it." And yet it made no impression on me. I might just as well have been under my poplar tree with a book. I turned to him and asked for a cigarette. He smiled.

"Feeling better?"

I began to laugh. "Yes, I feel better. I only wonder what I'm doing here with you."

"You're not doing anything; you're taking a drive, smoking a cigarette and wondering whether you won't be bored. Don't you want me to kiss you?"

He stopped the car, took me by the shoulders and gave me a kiss. There was no better means of recognition. I laughed a little, with his mouth on mine, and then we drove along, holding hands. He knew me through and through, and I had been living for the past two months with strangers who had settled down into a grief I did not share. Now life seemed to be slowly beginning again.

The sea was truly amazing. For a second I wished that Françoise could be there and I could tell her that, just as she had said, it was blue with red rocks and yellow sand, and the general effect was most satisfactory. I was afraid that Luc would point it out to me with a triumphal air and await my reaction, which would have forced me to summon up adjectives and a suitable pantomime. Instead, he just flicked a finger as we came into Saint-Raphael.

"There it is."

As we rolled slowly through the twilight, the sea turned from blue to a pale gray. At Cannes, Luc stopped the car on the Croisette, in front of an enormous hotel. The lobby terrified me. I knew that I could not be happy until I had forgotten this style of decoration and transformed these bellboys into human beings who would not frighten me by an excess of bowing and scraping. While Luc negotiated with a superior-looking man behind a desk, I wished that I could sink through the floor. He sensed my embarrassment and laid his hand on my shoulder to steer me to the elevator. The room was huge, almost white, with two French windows opening onto a view of the sea. There was a hubbub of porters and luggage, of closet doors and windows being thrown open. I stood with dangling arms, annoyed with myself for being so unexcited.

"Well, here we are," said Luc.

He cast a satisfied glance around the room and leaned over the balcony. I put my elbows up beside his, but at a respectful distance. I didn't feel in the least like looking at the view or being on intimate terms with a man whom I knew so slightly. He shot me a brief glance.

"Now you're unsociable again. Go take a bath and then come back here for a drink. According to my diagnosis, only comfort and alcohol can cheer you."

He was quite right. Once I had changed my dress, I

stood leaning over the balcony beside him, with a glass in my hand, and made agreeable remarks about the luxury of the bathroom and the beauty of the sea. He told me that I was looking my best, I returned the compliment in kind, and we looked with satisfaction at the palm trees and the crowd of people strolling below. Then he went off to change, in his turn, leaving me with a second glass of whisky, and I walked about barefoot on the heavy carpet, humming to myself.

Dinner went well. We spoke with tenderness and common sense about Françoise and Bertrand. I said how I should hate to run into Bertrand, and Luc assured me that we were certain to meet somebody who would take pleasure in telling Françoise and Bertrand the whole story. No use worrying about that until the holidays were over. I was touched by the fact that he should have run this risk for my sake and told him so with a yawn, because I was very sleepy. I also told him that I liked the way he took the whole thing.

"You're wonderful, really! You make up your mind to do something, you do it, you accept the consequences and you aren't afraid."

"Why should I be afraid?" he asked with strange melancholy. "Bertrand won't kill me; Françoise won't leave me. You won't love me."

"But Bertrand may kill *me*," I said with annoyance.

"He's much too nice. Everyone's nice, for that matter."

"Bad people are even more boring, you told me so yourself!"

"Quite right. And now it's very late; come along to bed."

He said this in the most natural manner. Our conversations were anything but romantic, but this "come along to bed" sounded a little offhand to me. To tell the truth, I was frightened, very much frightened of the night to come.

I put on my pajamas in the bathroom with trembling fingers. They were rather schoolgirlish pajamas, but they were all I had. When I came into the room, Luc was already in bed. His face was turned toward the window and he was smoking a cigarette. I slipped in beside him and he quietly took my hand. I was shivering all over.

"Take off those pajamas, silly. You'll rumple them. How can you be cold on a night like this? Are you ill?"

He took me in his arms, carefully removed my pajamas, rolled them up in a ball and threw them on the floor. I remarked that they would be rumpled, just the same. He began to laugh gently. All his gestures were incredibly gentle. Deliberately he kissed my mouth and shoulders, and went right on talking.

"You smell of warm grass. Do you like this room? Otherwise we'll go somewhere else. Cannes is rather a pleasant place. . . ."

I answered "Yes, yes," in a strangled voice, wishing it were tomorrow morning. It was only when he drew away from me a little and put his hand on my hip that I began to feel stirred. He caressed me, and I kissed his neck, his body, everything I could touch of this shadow profiled against the nocturnal sky. Finally he slipped his legs between mine, I slipped my hands over his back and we both gave a long sigh. Then I lost sight of him and of the sky of Cannes as well. I was dying, I was surely going to die, but I didn't die, I only fainted. Nothing else mattered: how could anyone fail to remember this forever? When we separated, Luc opened his eyes and smiled. I fell asleep immediately, with my head against his arm.

Chapter 2

I HAD always been told that it was very difficult to live with another person. I agreed, in theory but not in practice, during the brief time I spent with Luc. I agreed because I could never be really relaxed in his presence; I was afraid he might be bored. Heretofore I had always been more afraid of being bored by other people than I was of boring them, and this reversal of roles caused me a certain amount of worry. Yet how could it be difficult to live with someone like Luc, who said very little, never asked questions (especially not: "What are you thinking about?"), always looked happy to have me around and gave vent to none of the whims of either indifference or passion? We had the same gait, the same habits and lived in the same rhythm; our bodies suited each other, and all was well. I had no right to regret his failure to make the tremendous effort required of love, the effort to know and shatter the solitude of another. We were lovers and friends. We swam together in the too-blue Mediterranean, ate lunch almost without talking because we were dazed by the sun, and went back to the hotel.

Sometimes, as I lay in his arms in the moment of great tenderness that follows love-making, I wanted to say: "Luc, love me, let's try, allow us to try." But I did not say it; I confined myself to kissing his forehead, eyes, mouth, everything that stood out in this new face, the sensitive face that the lips discover after the eyes. I had never loved a face so much. I loved even his cheeks, although cheeks had always seemed to me the most lifeless and fish-like part of anyone's face. I pressed my face against Luc's cool cheeks, which had just a suspicion of beard to roughen them. I understood why Proust had written at such length about those of Albertine. And Luc, in turn, made me rediscover my own body, talking of it with interest, but without indecency, as if some precious object were under discussion. Yet sensuality was not the keynote of our relations; it was something quite different: a sort of cruel alliance against the weariness of sham and pretense and rhetoric, against . . . plain weariness.

After dinner we always went to the same bar, a slightly shady spot back of the Rue d'Antibes. It had a small orchestra, and the first time we went there Luc asked for *Lone and Sweet*, a song I had mentioned to him.

"That's what you like, isn't it?" he asked triumphantly.

"Yes, how thoughtful of you."

"Does it remind you of Bertrand?"

I said that it did, a little, that it had been for some time now in the juke boxes. He seemed annoyed.

"Too bad. But we'll find something else."

"Why?"

"Well, when you have an affair, you want to choose a certain tune, a certain scent and other such landmarks, for future memories."

I must have had an odd expression, for he began to laugh.

"No young person thinks about the future. But I'm building up an agreeable old age for myself, with the aid of records."

"Do you have quite a lot of them?"

"No."

"Too bad," I said angrily. "If I were your age, I'd have a whole collection."

Cautiously he took my hand.

"Hurt your feelings?"

"No," I said wearily. "But it's a little strange to think that, in a year or two, a whole week of your life, a living week, spent with a man, will amount to no more than a record. Especially if the man has proclaimed the fact in advance."

To my great irritation, I could feel tears well up in my eyes. It was all because of the way he had asked: "Hurt your feelings?" When people spoke to me in a certain tone of voice, I always felt like wailing.

"Aside from that, my feelings aren't hurt," I said nervously.

"Come," said Luc, "let's dance."

He took me in his arms and we danced to Bertrand's tune, which, actually, the orchestra here didn't play nearly as effectively as the recording. As we danced, Luc suddenly held me very tight, with what is probably called desperate tenderness, and I clung to him with the same desperation. Then he slackened his embrace and we talked about other things. We found a tune of our own, or rather it forced itself upon us, because everywhere we went we heard it.

Apart from this slight set-to, I behaved very well. I was gay and found our little affair entirely successful. And then, I admired Luc; I couldn't help admiring his intelligence and stability and the masculine way he had of seeing things in their true proportions, without either cynicism or indulgence. But every now and then I wanted to break out and say: "Look here, why don't you love me? I should feel so much more peaceful. Why not put up that pane of glass called passion between us? It may distort things at times, but it's wonderfully convenient." But no, we were two of a kind, allies and accomplices. In terms of grammar, I could not become the object, or he the subject. He had neither the capacity nor the desire to define our roles in any such way.

*   *   *

The week which he had staked out for us to spend together was gone, but Luc said nothing about going away. We were very tan, and our faces were drawn with lack of sleep from nights spent talking and drinking in the bar until dawn came up white over an inhumanly silent sea where all the boats were riding at anchor, while the maddest and most exclusive sea gulls were dozing under the eaves of the hotel. In the lobby, the same sleepy elevator boy was there to greet us, and Luc would take me in his arms to make love in a state of dizzy fatigue. Then we would wake up the following noon to go swim in the sea.

That morning—which should have been the last—I thought he loved me. He wandered about the room with an intriguingly reticent air.

"What did you tell your family? When did you say you'd be back?"

"I said in about a week."

"We can stay another week here, if you like."

"Yes. . . ." I said.

I realized that so far I hadn't really faced the necessity of going away. My whole life was to slip by, as if on an ocean cruise, amid the easily accepted comforts of this big hotel. With Luc, all my nights would be sleepless. We should drift slowly toward winter, toward death, continuing all the while to talk about a temporary situation.

"I thought Françoise was expecting you."

"That can be fixed," he said. "I don't feel like leaving Cannes. Neither Cannes nor you."

"Neither do I," I echoed in the same quiet, restrained voice.

Yes, the same voice. For a second I fancied that he loved me and didn't want to say so. Then I remembered that these were just words, part of the rhetoric which we had rejected, together. He was fond of me, and that was quite enough. We were simply allowing ourselves another week of having a very good time. After that, I must leave him. Leave him. . . . Why?—for whom?— for what? To return to my old loneliness and boredom and instability? At least when Luc looked at me, I saw him, and when he spoke I wanted to understand what he was saying. He took me out of myself and made me care for him and his happiness. For him, for Luc, my lover.

"It's a good idea," I continued. "As a matter of fact, I hadn't really thought about our going away."

"You never think about anything," he said, laughing.

"Not when I'm with you."

"Why? Do you feel young and irresponsible?"

He looked at me with a slight mocking smile. If I had taken him up on the "little girl and sugar-daddy" aspect of our relationship, he would have demolished it in no time flat. Fortunately I was feeling entirely adult. Adult and blasé.

"No," I replied, "I feel absolutely responsible. But responsible for what? My own life? It's malleable enough. I can handle it. I'm not unhappy. I'm contented. I'm not even happy. I'm just nothing, except that I feel exactly right when I'm with you."

"That's perfect," said Luc. "And I feel exactly right with you."

"Then let's purr."

He began to laugh.

"You spit like a cat as soon as anyone takes away

your daily dose of absurdity and despair. I don't care about making you 'purr.' Or about your being blissfully happy. That would be a bore."

"Why?"

"Because I'd be lonely. That's the one thing that frightens me about Françoise—to have her beside me, not opening her mouth and perfectly happy. Of course, from a masculine and social point of view, it's a satisfying accomplishment to make a woman happy, even if you don't know why."

"Then it's a perfect balance," I said abruptly. "You have Françoise to make happy and me to make unhappy, when this little jaunt is over."

I had no sooner said these words than I regretted them.

"You, unhappy?" he echoed, turning toward me.

"No," I answered, with a smile. "Just at loose ends, that's all. I'll have to find somebody else to take care of me, and no one will ever be as good at it as you."

"When the time comes, I don't want to be told about it," he said angrily. Then he changed his mind. "Yes, I do want to be told. You must tell me everything. If the fellow's unpleasant, I'll give him a thrashing. Otherwise, I'll speak well of him. In fact, I'll behave like a real father."

He took my hand, turned it over and planted a long, tender kiss on the palm. I laid my other hand on the nape of his neck as he bent down. This man who had suggested a short-lived, unsentimental adventure was, at bottom, young and vulnerable and good. Above all, he was honest.

"We're fundamentally honest," I said sententiously.

"Yes," he said, "but don't smoke your cigarette like that, if you want to pass for being respectable or honest!"

I drew myself up in my polka dot dressing gown.

"How can I be called an honest woman?" I exclaimed. "What am I doing rigged out like a streetwalker, with another woman's spouse in this decadent hotel? Am I not a typically vicious little existentialist girl from one of the cafés around Saint-Germain-des-Prés, the kind that breaks up a marriage without even putting her mind on it?"

"And what about me?" Luc joined in. "The model husband, carried away by lust, when the dangerous age came upon him . . . the solid citizen led around by the nose . . . by the nose, I tell you. . . . Come to me, darling!"

"Nothing doing! All I'm after is your money! Having roused your lustful desire, I refuse to appease it! There! Take that!"

He sank onto the bed, holding his head between his hands, and I solemnly sat down beside him. When he raised his head I stared hard at him.

"I'm a vamp!"

"And what am I?"

"An outcast! The wreck of what was once a man! . . . Oh, Luc, one more week!"

I flung myself down beside him and mingled his hair

with mine. He felt burning hot and fresh against my cheek, with a smell of salt water about him. . . .

*   *   *

I was alone, not without a certain feeling of satisfaction, in a deck chair in front of the hotel, facing the sea. Alone with a few old English ladies. It was eleven o'clock in the morning and Luc had gone to attend to some business in Nice. I rather liked Nice, or at least the shabby side of it between the station and the Promenade des Anglais. But I hadn't gone with Luc because I had a sudden urge to be alone.

I was alone, exhausted by lack of sleep, yawning my head off and feeling wonderfully well. I couldn't light a cigarette without my hand trembling. The September sun, no longer very hot, caressed my cheek. For once, I felt on very good terms with myself. "We feel really all right only when we're dead tired," Luc had said. Yes, I was one of those people who can't be at rest until they've killed off a certain amount of their own vitality, the part that drives them on and at the same time carries the germ of boredom, the part that asks: "What have you done with your life? What do you want to do?" This was a question to which I could only answer: "Nothing."

A handsome young man went by and I looked him over with an indifference that surprised me. As a rule, or at least up to a certain point, good looks gave me a feeling of discomfort. They seemed to me both indecent and inaccessible. This young man was easy on the eyes and, as far as I was concerned, utterly unreal. Luc obliterated all other men in my sight. But I didn't obliterate other women in his. He looked at them with obvious pleasure, even if he didn't put his appraisal into words.

Suddenly a mist came between me and the sea. I felt as if I were choking, and when I raised a hand to my forehead it was streaming with perspiration. The roots of my hair were drenched, and a drop slipped slowly down my back. Death was probably something like this: a bluish mist before the eyes and a sensation of falling through space. If I had really been dying, I should not have struggled against it.

I caught at this last phrase as it skimmed across my consciousness: "I should not have struggled against it." And yet I dearly loved a number of things: Paris, books, certain scents, love-making, and my present life with Luc. I had a premonition that I would never be so very much all right with anyone as I had been with Luc, that we were meant for each other. But fate further demanded that Luc should leave me and I should have to begin all over with somebody else. I would, of course, but there was no chance of its being the same thing; never again could I possibly lose my loneliness, say what I thought and enjoy such deep-seated calm. But Luc was going back to his wife, leaving me to interminable afternoons in my boardinghouse room, to fits of despair and liaisons that were bound to come to bad ends. I started to cry with self-pity.

Three minutes later I blew my nose. Two deck-chairs away, an old English lady stared at me, quite unmercifully, but with an interest that made me blush. I stared back at her, and for a second she inspired me with respect. She was a human being, like myself, and we stared at each other in the sunlight as if we were both dazzled by a kind of revelation. Two human beings who did not speak the same language staring at each other with mutual amazement. Then she got up and limped off, leaning on her cane.

Happiness has no history. And so this period in Cannes has left no clear imprint on my mind except for these few unhappy moments, Luc's laughter and the stale odor of summer mimosa in our room at night. Perhaps, for people like myself, happiness is a negative thing, an absence of worries, an absence filled with trust. At present I was experiencing this absence, and also, at times, when I met Luc's glance, the feeling that, at last, all was well. He was bearing my burden and looking at me with a smile. I knew why and wanted to smile back.

I remember, from one morning, a moment of particular exaltation. Luc was lying on the beach and I was diving from a raft. I climbed to the highest diving board and looked down at Luc, amid the crowd on the beach, and then at the water complacently waiting for me below. I was going to plunge and bury myself in it, I was going to fall from a very great height and during my fall I should be mortally alone. Luc looked at me and made a gesture of mock terror as I let myself go. The sea darted up to meet me and I hurt myself when I struck it. I swam back to shore and collapsed beside Luc, sprinkling him with sea water; then I laid my head against his dry back and kissed his shoulder.

"Are you crazy . . . or simply an incurable sportswoman?" Luc asked.

"Crazy."

"That's what I thought, with considerable pride, about you. When I said to myself that you were diving from such a great height to join me, I was very happy."

"Are you happy? I am. At least, I must be, since I don't have to stop and ask myself the question. That's an axiom, isn't it?"

I spoke without looking at him, for he was stretched out on his stomach and I could see only the tanned, firm back of his neck.

"I'm sending you back to Françoise in top-notch condition," I said jokingly.

"Cynic!"

"Women are notoriously cynical! Between Françoise and myself, you're just a little boy."

"Now you're pretentious!"

"There, men take the palm. A pretentious woman lends herself to ridicule. But a man's pretentiousness gives him a deceptive air of virility, which he cultivates in order to . . ."

"Haven't you perpetrated enough axioms by now? Talk about the weather! During the summer holidays no other topic is allowed."

"It's gorgeous," I said, "perfectly gorgeous. . . ." And then I rolled over onto my back and fell asleep.

When I woke up, the sky was overcast and the beach empty. I felt exhausted and my mouth was dry. Luc was sitting beside me, all dressed, puffing at a cigarette and looking out to sea. I lay there for a moment without letting him know I was awake, experiencing for the first time purely objective curiosity. "What can this man be thinking about? What can any human being think about on an empty beach, facing an empty sea, beside someone who is sleeping?" I felt as if he must be so crushed by these three absences that I held out my hand and touched his arm. He did not even start. He never started, rarely showed surprise and even more rarely offered any protest or objection.

"So you're awake?" he asked lazily, stretching with obvious reluctance. "It's four o'clock."

"Four o'clock!" I exclaimed, sitting up. "I've slept for four hours."

"Don't let that bother you," said Luc. "We have nothing to do."

These words had an ominous sound. It was true that we had nothing to do together, no shared work, no mutual friends.

"Do you mind?" I asked.

He turned toward me with a smile.

"I like nothing better. Put on your sweater, darling, or you'll be cold. We'll go have tea at the hotel."

The Croisette was gloomy without the sun, its old

palm trees swaying slightly in a feeble-hearted breeze. The hotel was asleep, and we had tea brought up to our room. I took a hot bath and then lay down on the bed beside Luc who was reading a book and intermittently flicking the ashes from his cigarette. We had drawn the blinds in order to shut out the sad sky, and the room was dimly lit, and hot. I lay on my back with my hands folded across my stomach, like a corpse or a fat man, and my eyes were closed. A faint rustle as Luc turned the pages of his book was all that interrupted the faraway sound of the breakers.

I said to myself: "Here I am, by Luc, close beside him, so close that I can touch him by merely reaching out my hand. I know his body, his voice, the way he sleeps. He's reading, I'm a little bored, and it's not at all unpleasant. Shortly, we'll have dinner, then we'll sleep together, and in three days we'll say good-by. He'll probably never again be the way he is now. But this moment is here; it's ours. I don't know whether it's love or just understanding, but that doesn't matter. We're alone, each one on his own. He doesn't know I'm thinking about us; he's reading. But we're together, and I'm hugging both the portion of warmth and the portion of indifference which he has given me. When we are separated, six months from now, the memory of this moment won't be the one to come back; there will be others, stupid and purely accidental. Yet this is probably the moment that I shall have liked best, the one in which I accepted the fact that life was as it now seems: calm and heart-rending."

I stretched out an arm to pick up *La famille Fenouillard*, a children's book which Luc had reproached me for not having read, and laughed over it until Luc wanted to join in my laughter. We bent over the same page, cheek to cheek and soon mouth to mouth; then the book fell onto the floor while pleasure descended upon us and night upon the world outside.

*   *   *

The day of our departure came at last. Hypocritically enough, we made no mention of it in the course of the evening before, which was to be our last one together. Our hypocrisy was nine-tenths fear: Luc's fear that I might give way to emotion, my fear that, knowing what was on his mind, I might actually live up to his fearful expectations. I woke up several times in the night, in a sort of panic, and searched for Luc with my head and hand, to make sure that our precious partnership in sleep still existed. Each time, as though he were on the watch for such terrors and his own sleep had been purposefully lightened, Luc took me in his arms, patted me and murmured in a strange voice: "There, there!"—as if to comfort an animal. It was a confused, whispering night, heavy with warmth, somnolence and the scent of the mimosa, which we were about to leave behind us. After that came morning, breakfast and the moment when Luc decided to pack his bags. I packed mine at the same time, talking about roads, restaurants along the roads and so on. I was a little annoyed by my own deceptively calm, brave voice, for I didn't feel at all calm and brave and saw no reason why I should. Actually I felt nothing at all, except, perhaps, a vague bewilderment. For once, we were putting on a sort of act for our mutual benefit, and I thought it wise to stick to it, since it was quite possible that I should really suffer before we finally said good-by. Better far to retain the gestures of restraint and decency.

"Well, we're ready," Luc said at last. "I'll ring for someone to come take down the bags."

I had a conscientious qualm.

"Let's lean for the last time over the balcony," I said in an appropriately melodramatic tone.

Luc looked at me anxiously and then, catching my expression, began to laugh.

"You're a tough little thing, a real cynic. I like you."

He had taken me in his arms in the middle of the room and was shaking me gently.

"It's very rare, you know, after two weeks of co-habitation, to say to someone: 'I like you.' "

"This wasn't cohabitation," I protested laughingly. "It was a honeymoon."

"All the more reason!" he exclaimed, letting me go. At that moment I really felt that he was leaving me and wanted to hold him back by the lapels of his coat. It was a most disagreeable fleeting impression.

The return journey went well. I drove part of the way. Luc said that we would reach Paris that night and he would ring me up the next day. Soon I must have dinner with him and Françoise, as she would be back from the two weeks she had spent in the country with her mother. All this seemed to me slightly alarming, but Luc said all I had to do was watch my tongue and make no reference to our trip, and he would take care of the rest. I could easily imagine myself spending the autumn in their company, occasionally meeting Luc to kiss his mouth and sleep with him. I had never entertained the idea that he should leave Françoise—first, because he had told me he'd never do it and second, because I couldn't see treating her that way. At that moment, even if he had offered to leave her, I don't believe that I should have accepted.

He told me that he had a lot of work to catch up with, but it didn't interest him particularly. As for me, another year of study lay ahead, and the necessity of delving deeper into subjects which had bored me the year before. In short, we returned to Paris in a mood of depression. But this rather pleased me; it meant that each one of us was depressed and bored in the same way and therefore felt the same need to cling to the other, to whom he was spiritually akin.

We reached Paris very late that night. At the Porte d'Italie I looked at Luc's weary face and reflected that we had come out of our little adventure very well, that we were civilized, reasonable adults. . . . Then, all of a sudden, I had a feeling of angry humiliation.

PART THREE

Chapter 1

I HAD no need to renew my acquaintance with Paris after I had once and for all discovered it. But I was astonished by its charm and the pleasure I found in walking through streets that had retained the vacant look of summer. This distracted me for three days from the emptiness and absurdity of my separation from Luc. I looked for him at night, sometimes groped for him with my hand, and each time his absence seemed stupid and unnatural. Already the two weeks we had spent together had taken shape and tone in my memory, and the tone was full and harsh at the same time. Strangely enough, I had a feeling not of failure, but, on the contrary, of success. A success which, as I realized all too well, would make any other similar attempt not only difficult but also painful.

Bertrand would be in Paris soon, and what was I to say to him? He would try to get me back, I felt quite sure. But why should I take up with him again? How could I bear the contact of a body and breath that did not belong to Luc?

Luc did not call me up the next day or even the day after. I put this down to complications with Françoise, and it gave me a twofold sensation of shame and importance. I took to long walks and to thinking with detachment and a very vague interest of the coming academic year. Perhaps I might find something to study that was better suited to me than law, since Luc had promised to introduce me to one of his friends who was a newspaper editor. The sheer inertia which so far had prompted me to look for sentimental compensations now seemed to point to the possibilities of a career.

After two days, I could no longer resist my desire to see Luc. Since I was afraid to telephone, I sent him an airy little note, asking him to call me, which he did the next day. He had gone to bring Françoise back from the country, and that was the reason why he had not called before. His voice sounded tense. I thought that he missed me, and for a second, just as he was telling me so, I had a vision of our meeting in a café, where he would take me in his arms and insist that, after the absurdity of these two days, he could not live without me. I had only to answer, without telling too much of an untruth: "Neither can I," and then allow him to decide what was to follow. But although he really did make an appointment to meet me in a café, it was simply to inform me that Françoise was well and had asked no questions, and that he was up to his ears in work. He said: "You're lovely," and kissed the palm of my hand.

I found him changed—perhaps because he had gone

back to wearing a dark suit—and altogether desirable. Looking at his clear-cut, tired face, I thought how curious it was that he no longer belonged to me. At the same time I reflected that I had not known how to "benefit" (odious word!) from our trip. I talked gaily and he answered in the same tone, but without spontaneity. Perhaps we were both surprised that it should have been so easy to live with someone for two weeks, to have it go off so well, with no serious consequences. But when he got up to leave, I felt like asking indignantly: "Where are you going? Surely you aren't going to leave me alone!" But that is exactly what he did, and I had nothing before me. I thought: "All this is ridiculous," and shrugged my shoulders. I walked about for an hour and went into one or two cafés in the hope of seeing someone I knew, but nobody was back. I could always spend a couple of weeks with my family, but as I was to dine with Luc and Françoise two days later, I decided not to go before then.

I spent these two days at the movies or on my bed, reading and sleeping. My room felt foreign to me. Then, on the evening of the dinner, I dressed carefully and went to their house. As I rang the bell, I had a moment of fright, but Françoise opened the door and her smile was immediately reassuring. I knew, as Luc had said, that she could never be ridiculous or play a part out of keeping with her natural kindliness and dignity. The idea that her husband could be unfaithful simply never entered her mind, or if it did she rose above it.

The dinner was a curious affair. Just the three of

us, and it went off just as successfully as ever before. Of course, we had drunk a good bit before sitting down at the table. Françoise seemed to know nothing, although I fancied she might be looking at me a little more attentively than usual. Luc talked to me from time to time, with his eyes on mine, and I felt bound to answer gaily and naturally. The conversation turned to Bertrand, who was to return to Paris the following week.

"I shan't be here," I said.

"Where will you be?" asked Luc.

"I'm probably going to spend a few days with my parents."

"And when will you be back?" This question was from Françoise.

"In two weeks."

I returned her glance, a trifle uneasily, but determined not to appear to avoid it. As Luc went over to the record-player, she laid her hand on mine for a second with a pathetic little smile.

"You'll send me a post card, Dominique, won't you? By the way, you never did tell me how you found your mother."

"Mother's well," I said. "She's . . ."

I stopped short because Luc had put on the song we had heard so often on the Riviera. With a rush everything came back to me. Luc did not turn around, and I was seized with panic. What did it all mean, my presence between this couple, the music, Françoise's indulgence, or apparent indulgence, Luc's sudden display

of a sentimentality which I knew was equally deceiving?
I had an almost irresistible impulse to run away.

"I like this tune," said Luc coolly.

He sat down, and I realized that he had no ulterior
motive whatsoever, no memory even of the sharp words
we had exchanged on the subject of a record collection.
The tune had haunted him and he had bought the record
simply in order to escape from its persecution.

"I like it, too," I said.

He raised his eyes to look at me, and then he did
remember. He smiled at me with such obvious tenderness that I had to stare at the floor. Françoise did nothing but light a cigarette. I was completely at sea. There
was no falsity about the situation, for it seemed to me
that if it were to be openly discussed each one of us
would give an objective and detached opinion.

"Are we going to the theater or not?" asked Luc,
turning to me to explain: "We have an invitation to see
a new play. There's no reason why all three of us
shouldn't go."

"Oh, yes!" I exclaimed. "Why not?" And I nearly
added, with an hysterical giggle: ". . . Considering how
things stand!"

Françoise took me to her room to fit me with one of
her coats, dressier than mine. She tried first one and then
another, swung me around and turned up the collars. At
a certain point she held my face between the collar ends
and I thought, with the same stifled laughter: "I'm at
her mercy. Perhaps she's going to throttle or bite me."
But she simply smiled.

"You look a little lost in this one."

"Quite true," I said, not thinking of the coat.

"I want to see you when you get back from your family's."

"Now I'm in for it!" I thought. "Is she going to ask me not to see Luc again? Can I do it?" And the answer was self-evident: "No, I can't, now."

"I've decided to take you in hand," she went on, "to dress you properly and open your eyes to things that are more amusing than books and bookworms."

"Good God!" I thought. "This offer is anything but well timed!"

"No?" she asked, as I did not reply. "I had a feeling you were a little bit my daughter." She laughed as she said this, but benevolently. "But if it's a mulish and strictly intellectual daughter . . ."

"You're really too kind," I said, stressing the "too." "I don't know what to do."

"Just leave it up to me," she said, laughing.

"Now I'm in a pretty mess," I thought. "But if Françoise is fond of me and wants to have me around, then I'll be able to see Luc more often. Perhaps, after ten years of marriage, she doesn't really care."

"Why do you like me?" I asked.

"Because you have the same temperament as Luc's. A restless, unhappy temperament that is fated to find consolation in persons born under the influence of Venus, like myself. You can't escape me! . . ."

I mentally threw up my hands. Then we went to the theater. Luc talked and laughed; Françoise pointed out various people and informed me of the connections between them. When they took me back to my boardinghouse, Luc kissed the palm of my hand in the most natural way in the world. I went to my room, somewhat in a daze, fell asleep and the next day took a train for my parents' place on the Yonne River.

Chapter 2

THE Yonne was gray and the boredom quite intolerable. The boredom was no longer abstract; it stemmed from the longing to be with one particular person. After a week I went back to Paris. My mother came to abruptly, just as I was leaving, and asked me whether I was happy. I said yes, that I enjoyed studying law, worked hard and had good friends. She relapsed, with a quieted conscience, into her melancholia. The year before, I should have wanted to confide in her, but now I had nothing to say. Decidedly, I was growing older.

At the boardinghouse I found a note from Bertrand, asking me to call him up as soon as I returned. It was obvious that he wanted an explanation—for I couldn't be at all sure that Catherine had held her tongue—and after all, he was entitled to it. I called him and we made an appointment. Meanwhile I signed up for meals at the university dining room.

At six o'clock I met Bertrand at the café on the Rue Saint-Jacques, and for a moment it seemed as if nothing had happened and we were beginning all over. But I was recalled to reality when he got up and kissed me solemnly on the cheek. Like a coward, I put on a light, irresponsible air.

"You're much handsomer," I said, quite sincerely, but with a cynical footnote addressed to myself: "My worse luck!"

"So are you," he said briefly. "I want you to know that Catherine has told me the whole story."

"What story?"

"About your trip to the Riviera. A couple of cross-checks have led me to think you were with Luc. It's so, isn't it?"

"Yes," I said. I was impressed by his behavior. He did not look furious, just calm and a little sad.

"Well, then, here it is. . . . I'm not the kind of man to share you with someone else. I still love you enough to wipe this off the slate. But not enough to suffer over you the way I did last spring. You'll have to choose."

He reeled off this ultimatum in a rapid but expressionless manner.

"Choose what?" I asked. It was very tiresome. Just as Luc had foreseen, I had never considered Bertrand as entering into the problem.

"Either you stop seeing Luc and we go on as usual. Or you go on seeing him, and we remain good friends. That's all."

"Of course," I said, "of course."

I couldn't think of a thing to say. Bertrand seemed grave and more mature; I almost admired him. But he was nothing to me now, absolutely nothing. I laid my hand on his.

"I'm dreadfully sorry," I said, "but I can't."

He was silent for a moment and looked out the window.

"It's a little hard to take," he said.

"I hate making you suffer," I went on, and I was honestly distressed.

"This isn't the worst part of it," he said, as if to himself. "You'll see. Once you've made up your mind, it's plain sailing. It's only when you hang on . . ." He turned to me suddenly. "You love him?"

"Of course not," I said with irritation. "There's no question of love. We understand each other, that's all."

"Count on me if you get into a tight corner," he said. "And I think you will. You'll see: there's really nothing to Luc at all; he's just a sad intellectual."

I thought with a gust of joy of Luc's tenderness, his laughter.

"Believe me. Anyhow," he added in a sort of outburst of feeling, "I'll always stand by you, Dominique, you know that. You made me very happy."

We both felt like crying, he because he had hoped against hope and now it was all over; I because I felt as if I were putting out from a safe haven into a tossing sea. I got up and brushed his forehead with a kiss.

"Good-by, Bertrand. Forgive me."

"Go away," he said gently.

I left, completely demoralized. The year had got off to a bad start.

*   *   *

Catherine was waiting for me in my room, seated on the bed, with a tragic expression. She got up as I came in and held out her hand. I shook it halfheartedly and sat down.

"Dominique, I want to apologize. Perhaps I shouldn't have said anything to Bertrand. What do you think?"

I admired her for having the nerve to ask me such a question.

"It doesn't really matter," I said. "It might have been better for me to inform him myself, but it doesn't really matter."

"Good," she said with relief. There was a gleam in her eye as she sat down again on the bed. "Now tell me all about it!"

I was dumb with amazement, then burst out laughing.

"Catherine, really! You're beyond me! First you dismiss the subject of Bertrand—filed and forgotten—and with that out of the way you pass on to something more juicy!"

"Don't tease me," she said, playing the child. "Let me have the story!"

"There's no story," I answered dryly. "I spent two weeks with someone I like, on the Riviera. For various reasons, it ends right there."

"He's married?" she asked shrewdly.

"No. He's a deaf-mute. Now I must unpack my bag."

"I'm not worried," said Catherine. "I know that you'll tell me all about it."

"The worst of it is that I probably will," I thought as I opened my closet. "Some day when I have the blues. . . ."

"Well," she continued, as if it were a startling revelation, "I'm in love."

"Who is it?" I asked. "Oh, yes, the latest comer. . . ."

"Well, if you don't want to know . . ."

She went right ahead, without waiting for me to reply. With angry gestures I proceeded to straighten my things. "Why do I have such silly friends?" I wondered. "Luc couldn't possibly stand her. But what has Luc got to do with this? Anyhow, 'this' is my life, the only one I've got."

"To make a long story short, I love him," Catherine concluded.

"What do you mean by love?" I asked curiously.

"Oh, I don't know; love means thinking about a man, going out with him, liking him better than anyone else. Isn't that about it?"

"I wouldn't know," I said. "Maybe."

I had finished my tidying and I sat wearily down on the bed. Catherine became very kind.

"Dominique, dear, you're crazy. Your head's in the clouds. You might just as well come along with us this evening. I'm going out with Jean-Louis, of course, and one of his friends, a very nice fellow who's interested in literature. It'll do you good."

I didn't want to telephone Luc before the next day. I was tired. Life seemed to me like a gloomy vortex, with Luc at the center, more often than not its only element of stability. He alone could understand and help me. I needed him. Yes, I needed him badly. I could demand nothing of him, yet he was vaguely responsible. Of course he must never know. I must abide by the rules of the game, particularly since they cut across the rules laid down in the established pattern.

"All right," I said, "let's go out with Jean-Bertrand and his literary friend. But I don't give a hoot for intellect, Catherine. No, that's not true, but I care only for sad intellectuals. People who get off scot-free get on my nerves."

"It's Jean-Louis, not Jean-Bertrand," she protested. "And what do you mean by 'get off scot-free'? Get off from what?"

"From all this," I said melodramatically, waving my hand in the direction of the window, where the lowering pink and gray sky was a pale reflection of hell.

"This won't do," said Catherine anxiously, and she took my arm as she guided me down the stairs. After all, she was a good friend.

Jean-Louis was good looking, in a slightly suspect but not at all disagreeable manner. But his friend Alain was subtler and more amusing. His intelligence was characterized by an acid perversity and elasticity, which were totally lacking in Bertrand. We soon left

Catherine and her admirer, who displayed their passion in a way that was sadly out of place, at least in a café. Alain took me home, talking along the way about Stendhal and other writers to whom I hadn't given a thought in the last two years. He was neither repulsive nor handsome; he was just nothing. I took up his suggestion to lunch together two days later, hoping that Luc would not be free on the same day. As usual, everything converged upon Luc; the course of events depended on him, and not on me.

Chapter 3

IN short, I was in love with Luc and stated the fact to myself quite definitely on the first night that I spent with him again, in a hotel on the quays. He was lying on his back, after making love, with his eyes closed, talking to me. "Kiss me," he said, and I raised myself on one elbow to kiss him. But as I bent over I was swept by a feeling of nausea, together with the hopeless conviction that this face, this man were the only things that counted for me. And that the unbearable pleasure, the expectancy that kept me hovering over his lips, were indeed the pleasure, the expectancy of love. So I laid my head on his shoulder, without kissing him, and gave a little moan of terror.

"You're sleepy," he said, putting his hand on my back and laughing a little. "You're like a little animal; after making love, you're thirsty or sleepy."

"I was thinking how fond I am of you," I said.

"I'm fond of you, too," he said, patting my shoulder. "But if I haven't seen you for three days, you sound a little formal."

"I respect you," I said. "I respect and love you."

We laughed together.

"Seriously," I said abruptly, as if the idea had just crossed my mind, "what would you do if I really loved you?"

"But you really do love me, I know that," he said, with his eyes still closed.

"I mean, if you were indispensable to me, if I wanted you to myself, always? . . ."

"It would bother me," he said. "I certainly shouldn't find it flattering."

"And what would you say?"

"I'd say: 'Dominique, hm . . . Dominique, forgive me.' "

I sighed with relief. Thank God, he wasn't sanctimonious about it; he wouldn't say: "I told you so."

"I forgive you in advance," I replied.

"Give me a cigarette, will you," he said lazily. "They're on your side of the bed."

We smoked, without talking. I said to myself: "So I love him. Probably my love is just the idea 'I love him.' *That's* all there is to it, but outside of *that*, there's no salvation."

Certainly *that* had occupied the whole preceding week, ever since Luc's telephone call: "Will you be free on the night of the fifteenth?" Those words had echoed in my brain every three or four hours, in the same cold tone as he had spoken them, causing the balance within me to vacillate between happiness and suffocation. Now I was with him, and time went slowly and blankly by.

"I'll have to be going," he said. "It's late. Quarter to five."

"Yes," I said. "Is Françoise in town?"

"I told her I was going with some Belgians to Montmartre. But all the night clubs must be closed by now."

"What will she say? Five o'clock is late, all right, even for Belgians."

With his eyes still closed, he answered:

"When I get home, I'll yawn and say: 'Oh, those Belgians!' She'll turn over in bed and answer: 'There's some Alka-Seltzer in the bathroom.' And then she'll go back to sleep. You see!"

"Of course. And tomorrow you'll have to produce a whole rigmarole about night-club shows and the morals of Belgians, and . . ."

"Only a few names. I have no taste for telling lies, and no time, either."

"No time for what?"

"For anything. I haven't time, or strength or will. If I had anything in me at all, I'd have loved you."

"And would that have made any difference?"

"No, not for us; at least, I don't think so. Only I'd have been unhappy about you, instead of quite contented, as I am the way things are."

I wondered if this were not a caution in regard to

my questioning of a few minutes before. But he only laid his hand on my head in a solemn manner.

"I can say everything to you. It's a wonderful feeling. I never could tell Françoise that I don't really love her, that our marriage isn't based on any honest ideal. It's founded on my weariness and boredom. Although those are solid enough bases. Plenty of lasting marriages are built on them, God knows. At least, they're always present."

I raised my head from his shoulder. "They're just..." My whole being protested, and I was about to say: "... nonsense!" But something stopped me short.

"They're just what? Are you having a slight attack of youth?" And he gave a tender laugh. "My poor little dear, you're so young, so disarmed. And, fortunately, so disarming. That makes me feel easier in my mind."

He took me back to the boardinghouse. The next day I was to lunch with him and Françoise and one of their friends. Now I kissed him through the window of the car to say good-by. His face was drawn and old. This distressed me a little and, for the moment, made me love him the more.

Chapter 4

I WOKE up in high spirits the next day. Lack of sleep always agreed with me. I went over to the window, drank in the Paris air and lighted a cigarette for which I had no real craving. Then I went back to bed, after a glance at the mirror, which revealed dark circles under my eyes and an interesting expression. In fact, a face that inspired confidence and sympathy. I decided to ask the landlady to turn the heat on the very next day, because she was really carrying things too far.

"This room is freezing cold," I said aloud, and my voice had a hoarse, ludicrous sound.

"Dear Dominique," I added, "you're in love, you have a passion on your hands. That calls for treatment: walks, organized reading, young men, a little light work. Just what you need."

I had to give myself a certain amount of credit. I had a sense of humor, after all, and I felt very well. Apparently I flourished on passion. Besides, I was going to lunch with my flame. Armed with this frail detachment, due to a sense of physical well-being whose source I knew very well, I set out to see Luc and Françoise. I jumped onto a moving bus, and the conductor, under the pretext of bracing me, slipped his arm around my waist. I handed him the fare and we exchanged an understanding smile, because he was a ladies' man and I was a lady that knew what ladies' men were after. I stayed on the platform and leaned against the rail, while the bus jolted and ground the pavement below. Very well, I felt, very well, with a belt of insomnia that stretched all the way from my jaw to my solar plexus.

When I reached the house, the stranger who was to be the fourth member of our party was already there, a curt, red-faced, stoutish man. Luc was not present; Françoise told us that he had spent most of the night with some Belgian clients and had not got up until ten o'clock in the morning. The way those Belgians always insisted on being taken to Montmartre was so dreadfully boring! The fat man looked at me, and I blushed. Just then Luc came in, looking very tired.

"Ah, so it's you, Pierre. How goes it?"

"Weren't you expecting me?"

"Of course I was, old man," said Luc with a slightly irritated smile. "Isn't there anything to drink in these parts? What's that lovely yellow stuff in your glass, Dominique?"

"A light whisky," I answered. "Have you forgotten what it looks like?"

"No," he said, sitting down on the edge of an armchair, as if it were a bench in the waiting room of a railway station. Then he threw a glance at us, just the sort of absent, indifferent glance to be expected of a traveler. There was a childishly stubborn look on his face, and Françoise could not help laughing.

"Poor Luc, you look almost as badly as Dominique. Anyhow, my dear child, I'm going to put a stop to all this. I'm going to tell Bertrand that he . . ."

And she explained what she was going to tell Bertrand. I had not looked at Luc. Thank goodness, we never conspired to toss the ball back and forth between us in her presence. Even when we were alone together, strangely enough, we talked of her as if she were a beloved child who gave us some cause for anxiety.

"That kind of carousing doesn't agree with anyone," said the stoutish man, and I realized all of a sudden that probably he had seen us at Cannes and made a good guess about the night before. This explained the crusty look he had given me when we met, his curt manner and the undertones of what he was saying. Then I remembered that we *had* seen him at Cannes and that Luc had pointed him out as someone who had been interested in Françoise. He must be shocked and perhaps gossipy as well, devoted to the same principles as Catherine: never conceal anything from your friends, do them a good turn, don't let anyone take them in. . . . If Françoise were to find out, if she were to look at me with contempt and anger, sentiments so foreign to her, which I really didn't deserve . . . what would I do then?

"Let's go have lunch," said Françoise. "I'm starved."

We set out on foot for a restaurant near by. Françoise took my arm, and the men followed.

"It's very mild," she said. "I adore the autumn."

God knows why, this sentence quite irrelevantly roused a memory of the hotel room at Cannes, of Luc saying from the window: "Go take a bath and then come back here for a drink." He said that on the first day, when I was ill at ease, but then there were fifteen others to come, fifteen days and nights with Luc. . . . That was what I desired above everything else in the world at the present moment, and I should probably never have a second chance. If I had known . . . No, even if I had known, it would have been the same way. Proust has a sentence about that: "Happiness very rarely alights on the desire that called it." And yet this had happened, just the night before, when after a week of longing for it, I found myself close to Luc's face. This coincidence had given me a feeling of nausea, due perhaps to the sudden filling of the void of my normal existence, a void caused by the feeling that my life and I were not completely one. At that moment, on the contrary, I had the impression of complete unity and culmination.

"Françoise!" called Pierre from behind us.

We turned around and changed partners. I found myself walking ahead with Luc, keeping step with him along the russet-colored avenue. The same thought must have occurred to him, for he threw me a questioning, almost brutal glance.

"There you are," I said.

He shrugged his shoulders sadly, took a cigarette from his pocket, lit it and handed it to me. Whenever anything disturbed him, he could always fall back on a cigarette, although he had really no mannerisms or nervous habits of any kind.

"*He* knows . . . all about us," he said, jerking his head back to indicate Pierre. But he said it quietly, almost thoughtfully, with no apparent fear.

"Is it serious?" I asked.

"He won't be able to resist this chance to 'console' Françoise. But in this case, the 'consolation' isn't likely to go too far."

I admired his masculine smugness.

"He's a harmless idiot," Luc added, "one of Françoise's professor friends. Do you know the kind I mean?"

I did. Luc went on.

"All that bothers me is the hurt to Françoise. . . . The fact that it's you . . ."

"I quite see."

"It would bother me for you, too, if Françoise were to hold it against you. Françoise can do you a lot of good. She's a very sure friend."

"I haven't a sure friend," I said ruefully. "I have nothing sure."

"Sad?" he asked, taking my hand.

For a moment I was touched by this gesture and the risk it apparently involved, then sadness overpowered me. Yes, we were walking, hand in hand, under Françoise's very eye, but she knew Luc for exactly what he was, a tired man. Probably she thought that if he had anything on his conscience, he wouldn't give himself so easily away. No, the risk was actually very small. Luc was fundamentally indifferent. I squeezed his hand. Yes, this was Luc, and Luc was this, nothing more. The fact that "this" filled all my days never failed to astonish me.

"No, not sad," I replied. "Just nothing."

I lied. I wanted to tell him I was lying, that the truth was I needed him. But when I was with him, all this seemed unreal. There was nothing, nothing beyond fifteen days, and the imaginings and regrets they had left behind. Why should I be so cruelly torn? That was love's sorrowful mystery, I thought with contempt. I was angry with myself, because I knew I was sufficiently strong and free to have an affair that was happy.

Lunch lasted a long time. Looking at Luc upset me. He was handsome, and intelligent, and tired. I didn't want to give him up. I made vague plans for the winter ahead. When we separated he said he would ring me up. Françoise said she would ring me, too, with plans to take me to see somebody or other.

Neither of them did ring, and this silence lasted ten days. Luc's name weighed heavily upon me. Finally he rang up to say that Françoise knew everything and that he would see me as soon as he could, but he didn't know just when, for he was up to his ears in work. His voice was gentle. I stood quite still in the middle of the room, unable to take it all in. I was to have dinner with Alain, but he could do nothing for me. I felt bankrupt, done for.

I saw Luc twice in the two weeks that followed. Once at a bar on the Quai Voltaire, once in a hotel room where we found nothing to say to each other, either before or after. Things had a horrid taste of ashes. It is always curious to see to what extent life ratifies romantic conventions. I realized that I was definitely not cut out to be the gay little accomplice of a married man. I loved him. I should have thought of it before, or at any rate foreseen that love could be this insatiability, this obsession. I tried to laugh, but he did not respond. He talked gently, tenderly to me, as though he were going to die. . . . Françoise had taken it very hard indeed.

He asked me what I was doing. I said I was working, reading. But I never opened a book or went to a movie without looking ahead to the moment when I could talk to him about it. Often the writer or director was one of his friends. I attempted desperately to find links between us, other links besides the rather sordid grief we had inflicted upon Françoise. There was none to be found, although we never thought about remorse. I couldn't say: "Remember . . ." That would have been cheating. Besides, the effect would have been to scare him off. I couldn't say that I saw, or fancied I saw, his car all over town, that I repeatedly started to dial his telephone number without ever finishing, that I feverishly inquired of my landlady for messages when I came in, that everything reminded me of him, and that at the same time all this made me very angry. I was entitled to nothing. But nothing, at that moment, meant his face, and hands, and tender voice, all that unbearable past. . . . I lost weight every day.

Alain was kind, and one day I told him the whole story. We walked for miles, and he discussed my passion as if it were a literary subject, thus helping me to see it in the proper perspective and make the salutary effort of putting my thoughts into words.

"Just the same, you know it will be over some day," he said. "In six months or a year, you'll be joking about it."

"I don't want to," I said. "I'm defending not only myself, but everything we were together: the Cannes we knew, our secret laughter and understanding."

"But that shouldn't prevent your knowing that some day it will have lost all importance to you."

"I know it, but I can't feel it. I don't care about the future. Today, this minute, nothing else matters."

We kept on walking. He took me back to the boardinghouse and shook my hand gravely. When I went in I asked the landlady if Mr. Luc H. had called. She smiled and said no. I lay down on my bed and thought about Cannes.

I said to myself: "Luc doesn't love me," and that gave me a twinge of pain in the region of the heart. Every time I repeated this simple sentence, the pain came back, sometimes just as sharp as before. Then it seemed to me that I had made a step forward. The very fact that this little pain was at my orders, ready to appear promptly, armed to the teeth, as soon as I chose to call it, made me think that I had it under my control. I had only to say: "Luc doesn't love me," and this bewildering thing happened. But even if I did have a measure of control over it, I could not prevent its sudden eruption, during a class or a meal, with the full power to surprise and hurt me. No more than I could suppress the boredom of my shapeless, larval daily existence, the tired, rainy mornings, the deadly classes, the futile conversasations. I suffered, and told myself I was suffering, in an analytical or ironical way, any way at all to obliterate the lamentable evidence of an unhappy love.

The inevitable happened. I saw Luc again one evening. We drove through the Bois in his car and he said he had to go for a month to America. I said that was interesting; then the truth burst upon me. A month! I reached for a cigarette.

"When I get back, you'll have forgotten about me," he said.

"Why should I?"

"My poor darling, you'd be so much better off, so very much better. . . ." And he stopped the car.

I looked at him. His face was taut and grieved. So he knew. He knew exactly what I felt. He was no longer just a man, one whom I had to handle with care if I wanted him for a lover; he was a friend as well. Suddenly I clung to him, I laid my cheek against his, I looked at the shadows of the trees and found myself saying incredible things.

"Luc, I can't bear it. You mustn't leave me. I can't live without you. You've got to stay here. I'm so terribly alone. It's more than I can bear."

My own voice amazed me; it was a young, supplicating, indecent voice. I said to myself the things that Luc might have been saying: "Now, now; it'll all be over soon. Take it easy." But he made no sound and I went right on talking.

Finally, as if to check this flow of words, he took my head in his hands and gently kissed my mouth.

"My poor darling," he said, "my poor sweet. . . ."

There was real emotion in his voice. Two thoughts occurred to me together: "The time has come," and: "I'm very much to be pitied." I began to cry against his coat. Time was going by, and soon he would take me home, exhausted. I was allowing this to happen, and before I knew it he would be gone. Something in me rebelled.

"No," I said, "no."

I kept clinging, I wanted to melt into him, to disappear.

"I'll call you up. I'll see you again before I go," he was saying. "I'm sorry, Dominique, I'm sorry. . . . I've been so happy with you. You'll get over this. Time makes everything pass. I'd give anything to . . ."

He made a helpless gesture.

"To love me?" I asked.

"Yes."

His cheek was soft and hot from my tears. I wasn't going to see him for a month, and he didn't love me. How strange was despair, and how strange the recovery from it! He took me home, and I stopped crying. I was completely done in. He called me up the next day and the day after. The day he left I was in bed with grippe and he came to say good-by. Alain had dropped in, and Luc kissed me on the cheek, with the promise to write me a letter.

Chapter 5

SOMETIMES I woke up dry-mouthed, in the middle of the night, and before I completely came to, something whispered to me to go back to sleep, to sink back into the refuge of warmth and unconsciousness. But already I was saying to myself: "It's just that I'm thirsty; I'll get up, go to the wash-stand, drink some water and then sleep again." But when I was up, when I saw myself, vaguely reflected by a street lamp, in the mirror, when tepid water ran down my throat, I hurried back to bed, shivering. Once I lay flat on my stomach, with my head between my arms, and pressed my body flat against the bed, as if my love for Luc were a warm, deadly animal, which in a fit of rebellion I could crush between the sheet and my skin.

Then the battle began. Memory and imagination were ferocious enemies. There was Luc's face, Cannes, what had been, what might have been. And, without cease, the revolt of my body, which needed sleep; of my intelligence, which was sickened by the whole performance. I sat bolt upright and drew up my accounts: "This is me, Dominique, I love Luc, who doesn't love me. Unrequited love, inevitable sorrow. Break it up...." I imagined means of breaking definitely with Luc, for instance, by means of a well-turned, noble letter, explaining that everything was over. But this letter interested me only in so far as its polished style and nobility of thought brought Luc back to me. I no sooner saw myself separated from him by this cruel means than I began to imagine a reconciliation.

All you need to do is react, fight back, as people say. But for whose benefit? I wasn't interested in anyone else, or even in myself. I didn't interest myself except in relation to Luc.

Catherine, Alain, the streets; the young man who kissed me at a party, whom I refused to see again. The Sorbonne, rain, cafés, post cards from America. I loathed America. Boredom. Would all this ever end? Luc had been gone for over a month. He had written me a sad, tender little note, which I knew by heart.

One thing cheered me: my intelligence, which had opposed my passion unequivocally, laughing at it and me, and giving rise to strenuous mental debate, began to play a subtler role, as my ally. I no longer said to myself: "Let's stop this nonsense," but: "How can I limit the damage?" Nights were still bogged down in sadness, but reading made the days fly by. I pondered over the case of "Luc and Dominique," in clinical fashion, which did not eliminate certain unbearable moments when I stopped short on the sidewalk and a familiar sensation penetrated my being, filling me with disgust and anger. I would go to a café, put twenty francs into the juke box and treat myself to five minutes of melancholy, brought on by Luc's tune. Alain came to detest the song. But I knew every note, I remembered the scent of the mimosa; in short, I had my money's worth and disliked myself intensely.

"There, old thing," said Alain patiently, "there!"

I didn't much care to be called "old thing," but at the moment it was cheering.

"You're good to me," I said to Alain.

"No," he said. "I'm just using you. I'll write my thesis on passion."

But this music gave me one certainty. It convinced me that I needed Luc. I knew very well that this need was connected with my love and at the same time separated from it. In him I could still dissociate the human being, my friend, and the object of my passion, the enemy. The worst of it was that I couldn't underrate him, as one usually can people who respond inadequately. There were also times when I said to myself: "Poor Luc, what a burden I should be to him, what a nuisance!" And I despised myself for not having remained lighthearted. That might have attached him to me, out of sheer pique. But Luc didn't know what pique was. He wasn't an enemy; he was just Luc. I couldn't get away from it.

One day as I started off at two o'clock to a class, the landlady handed me the telephone receiver. My heart didn't quicken, because I knew Luc was still away.

Instantly I recognized the low, hesitant voice of Françoise.

"Dominique?"

"Yes."

The staircase was dead still.

"Dominique, I wanted to telephone you before this. Will you come to see me, just the same?"

"Of course," I said, controlling my voice to such a degree that it must have sounded unduly formal.

"Will you come at six this evening?"

"Certainly. I'll be there."

And she rang off. I was upset and glad to have heard her voice. It brought back memories of the week end at Bertrand's mother's, the car, a series of restaurant lunches and the settings in which we had moved together.

Chapter 6

I DIDN'T go to my class but walked about the streets wondering what Françoise would have to say. In keeping with the classical reaction, I felt that I had suffered too much for anyone to bear me ill will. It was drizzling at six o'clock, and the streets were wet and shiny in the lamplight, like the backs of seals. As I entered the hall of the apartment house I saw myself in a mirror. I had grown very thin, and had the vague hope that I might fall seriously ill and Luc would come to sob at my deathbed. My hair was wet, and I had a hunted air; no doubt I should arouse Françoise's never-failing kindness. I lingered there for a second, looking into the glass. Perhaps I could have played it a different way; I could have kept Françoise's affection and schemed to see Luc on the side. But how could I have schemed, when I was possessed for once by such a pure, unarmed, absolute passion? My own capacity for love had quite dazzled me. I forgot that it meant nothing, really, except an opportunity to suffer.

Françoise opened the door with the ghost of a smile and a mildly terrified air. I took off my raincoat as I walked in.

"How are you?" I asked.

"Very well," she answered. "Won't you sit down?"

The intimate manner which had come to exist among the three of us was gone. I sat down and she looked at me, visibly surprised by my lamentable appearance. This made me feel very sorry for myself.

"Will you have something to drink?"

"With pleasure."

Quite as a matter of course, she handed me a glass of whisky. I had forgotten the taste. Yes, life was quite a different proposition in my bleak living quarters and the university dining room. And the russet coat they had given me had come in very handy. I felt tense and desperate, yet my very state of nerves lent me self-assurance.

"Well, here we are," I said.

I raised my eyes to look at Françoise, who was sitting on a sofa directly across from me and staring at me without speaking. We could still talk on some quite extraneous subject, and when the time came for me to go I could say with a slightly embarrassed air: "I hope you don't hold it too much against me." It all depended on me. I had only to start talking before our silence became a double acknowledgment of what stood between us. But I did not say a word. At last I was living through a really significant moment.

"I meant to call you up before this," she said finally, "because Luc told me to do it. And then it worried me to think you were alone, here in the city. However . . ."

"I meant to call you, too," I answered.

"Why?"

I was about to say: "To apologize," but the term seemed too feeble. I began to speak the truth.

"Because I wanted to, because I was really lonely. And then because it worried me to think that you thought . . ." I made a vague gesture.

"You don't look well," she said gently.

"Exactly," I said angrily. "If I'd been able to, I'd have come to see you; you'd have made me eat steaks, I'd have stretched out on your rug and let you cheer me up. You were the one person that knew how, and yet the only one to whom I couldn't turn."

I trembled. My glass shook in my hand. Françoise's gaze had become unbearable.

"It was all very . . . unpleasant," I said apologetically.

She took the glass away from me, set it on the table and sat down again.

"I was jealous," she murmured. "I was physically jealous of you."

I looked at her. I had expected anything but that.

"It was silly of me," she said. "I knew perfectly well that what happened between you and Luc was nothing serious."

Seeing my expression, she made a quick gesture of apology, for which I gave her credit.

"I mean that unfaithfulness of a physical kind doesn't really matter. But I've always taken it hard, and particularly now . . . now . . . that . . ."

She seemed to be in pain, and I was afraid of what she might say.

"Now that I'm no longer so young," she went on, turning away her head, "nor so desirable."

"No," I said.

I protested. I had never thought that this affair could have another dimension, a dimension that was unknown to me, something pathetic, no, not even pathetic, just ordinary and sad. But then I knew nothing about their life together.

"That wasn't it," I said, getting up.

I went toward her and remained standing. She turned to me, smiling a little.

"My poor Dominique! What a mess!"

I sat down beside her, with my head between my hands and my ears buzzing. I felt quite empty and wanted to cry.

"I'm fond of you," she said, "very fond of you. I don't like to think you've been unhappy. When I first saw you, I thought we could change your slightly hangdog expression into something more gay. But the attempt hasn't been very successful."

"Oh, I've been unhappy, all right," I said. "But Luc warned me."

I wanted to crumple up against her big, generous body, to tell her I wished she were my mother, to reveal the full extent of my unhappiness, to let myself go and cry. But this role, too, was beyond my powers.

"He'll be back in another ten days," she said.

Why did a shock go through my obstinate heart? Françoise must recover Luc and her imperfect happiness. I must sacrifice myself. This last idea made me

smile; it was a last effort to conceal my own unim-
portance. I had nothing to sacrifice, not even hope. I
had only to end, or allow time to put an end to, an
illness. Such bitter resignation implied a certain amount
of optimism.

"Later on," I said, "when I'm entirely over it, I'll
see you again, Françoise, and Luc too. Now all I can
do is wait."

She kissed me gently at the door and said: "Good-by,
see you again soon."

But as soon as I was home, I threw myself upon my
bed. What cold-blooded nonsense had I said to her?
Luc was coming; he would take me in his arms and kiss
me. Even if he didn't love me, he, Luc, would be there.
This nightmare would be over.

*   *   *

Luc did come back, ten days later. I knew it, because
I went past his house on a bus the day of his return and
saw his car. I went back to my room and waited for
him to call me up. But he did not call, neither that day
nor the next when I stayed in bed pretending I had
the grippe, in order not to miss him.

He was there, and he did not call. After a month and
a half's absence. This shivering, this obsessed apathy,
this muffled laughter all added up to despair. Never
had I suffered so much. I told myself that this was the
last twinge, but it was a sharp one.

On the third day I got up and went to the Sorbonne.
Alain began taking walks with me again, I listened at-

tentively to what he said, and even laughed. For some unknown reason, I was obsessed by a quotation: "Something is rotten in the state of Denmark." These words were on my lips all the time.

On the fifteenth day I woke up to the sound of music in the courtyard, broadcast by a generous neighbor's radio. It was a lovely andante of Mozart's that always called up dawn, death, a certain smile. I lay motionless in bed for a long time, listening to it and feeling rather happy.

The landlady called me. Someone had asked for me on the telephone. Unhurriedly I slipped on a dressing gown and went down. I thought it must be Luc, and it didn't really matter. . . . Something had flowed out of me, fled.

"How are you?"

I listened to his voice, for it was his voice. How did I happen to feel such sweetness and calm, as though something living and essential were ebbing away? He asked me to have a drink with him the next day, and I said: "Yes, yes."

I went up to my room, all attention. The music was over, and I was sorry to have missed the end. I caught an unexpected glimpse of my face in the mirror, and saw myself smile. I didn't try to prevent it; besides, I couldn't have if I'd tried. Once more, and I knew it, I was alone. Alone. Alone. Well, what did it matter? I was a woman who had loved a man. It was a simple story.

THE END

Made in the USA
Monee, IL
21 August 2020